VOWED VENGEANCE

✳

Amanda bit her lower lip nervously. "I started to come on out, aimin' to help Ma. But she turned and I could tell in her eyes she wanted me to stay behind."

Amanda bit back the bile that rose in her throat. "They started slappin' Ma around some, hootin' and laughin'. . . ." She broke off again, her breath rattling in and out.

"You don't have to say it," Calhoun offered. He knew full well what Amanda was trying to say. It made knots of sickness in his stomach. He could not understand how men could do such a thing to a kindly woman like Mother Powell. He only knew that such men existed. And that he would have to try to make sure this particular group of them did not exist much longer.

Don't miss these other exciting books in the
Saddle Tramp series by Clint Hawkins

**SADDLE TRAMP #2: THE CAPTIVE
SADDLE TRAMP #3: GUNPOWDER TRAIL**

Coming Soon

**SADDLE TRAMP #4: GOLD AND LEAD
SADDLE TRAMP #5: BANDIT'S BLOOD**

Available from
HarperPaperbacks

SADDLE TRAMP

CLINT HAWKINS

HarperPaperbacks
A Division of HarperCollins*Publishers*

HarperPaperbacks   *A Division of* HarperCollins*Publishers*
                    10 East 53rd Street, New York, N.Y. 10022

Cover illustration by John Thompson

First printing: December 1991

Printed in the United States of America

HarperPaperbacks and colophon are trademarks of
HarperCollins*Publishers*

10 9 8 7 6 5 4 3 2

CHAPTER

* 1 *

Wade Calhoun felt no satisfaction as the blade of his bowie knife bit deep into his foe's ample supply of belly flesh and then chunked off the breastbone.

The man groaned, and sagged against Calhoun, whose knife was the only thing holding him up. Calhoun took a step backward and let the hefty man fall.

Calhoun ripped the knife free viciously. He spun, a snarl curling his thin lips.

Another man slammed into Calhoun, knocking him backward until his spine rammed the edge of the bar. The planks that formed the bar spilled off the big kegs on which they had rested and crashed to the dirt floor of the saloon.

The man's thin, vein-laced arms enveloped Calhoun, pinning them so that Calhoun was unable to make use of the big knife or one of his pistols.

"Damn your hide," Calhoun muttered.

He reared back and head-butted his opponent. His worn slouch hat went flying, revealing a tangled shock of dirty brown hair that needed a trim.

The man grunted with the impact, and relaxed his grip. Calhoun kicked him in the crotch. The man screeched in pain and turned pasty white.

Calhoun glanced at the others for an eye blink. Then he slammed the heel of his right hand into the man's forehead. The man's head snapped backward. He stumbled away a few steps, head lolling back on his scrawny, wrinkled neck.

Calhoun immediately stepped up. The swiftly arcing bowie flashed in the rancid saloon's dull, smoky lantern light. Suddenly a large, gaping slash appeared in the man's scarecrow-like throat. The devilish, nether smile spurted out fountains of blood, splattering Calhoun.

Calhoun snarled as five more men started moving toward him. Like the first two, Calhoun knew none of them. He flipped the knife up, caught the bloody blade in his hand and then flung it.

The twelve-inch blade sank hilt-deep in one man's chest. The man sank to his knees. He had been reaching for his pepperbox pistol, but stopped and looked at Calhoun with shock in his eyes and then pitched forward onto his face.

But Calhoun was not paying attention. One of the remaining men was scuttling for the door.

The three others—a huge bear of a man, a dull, oafish-looking fellow, and a sallow, mean-visaged man—were reaching for pistols.

The saddle tramp was faster and meaner. He had had his fill of these fine citizens of Broken Wheel. He had done nothing to offend them. He had simply been minding his own business, wanting a few drinks and a romp with one of the fallen angels. Then all this had happened.

Calhoun's two Colt Dragoon pistols popped into his

large, crusty hands.

"I'll gut shoot the next son of a bitch that moves on me," he growled.

The three men facing him froze, expressions of fearful hate darkening their eyes and faces.

The big one was usually looked on by the others as their leader. But now he was afraid. He licked his lips.

"You don't scare us none, sonny," he said, trying to sneer bravely. More than a little bit of a quiver in his voice betrayed his fear.

Calhoun said nothing. He just thumbed back the hammers of the two powerful .44-caliber Colt revolvers. And waited.

The three men stood trying to swallow their fear enough to make a play against this hard-eyed man with the brace of cap-and-ball Colts. They had seen what he had done to their two companions. They were afraid. They had been sure that with seven of them, this saddle tramp would have no chance. Suddenly the odds had diminished, and the men were not sure.

So they stood, watching.

Calhoun was fairly tall—a couple inches under six-foot—and thin as a rail. But the slimness could not hide the long, rope-like muscles, nor the deceptive strength they held. His razor-thin, acne-scarred face was covered with a few days' worth of stubble, and his hair not only needed trimming, it could also do with a good combing.

"What's your pleasure, boys?" Calhoun impatiently asked after a few moments.

One man, who had a tinge of craziness about him, Calhoun figured, twitched. His arms jerked.

Calhoun did not wait to see if it was a nervous afflic-
tion or whether the man was fixing to pull the old Colt
Paterson he had stuffed in the waistband of his worn
trousers. Calhoun simply drilled the jumpy little fellow
neatly through the forehead.

The other two men stood gaping in stunned shock
for several heartbeats. Then one went for his pistol;
the second spun and raced for the door.

"Hell," Calhoun muttered unemotionally as he calmly fired the Dragoons. First the one in his right hand,
then the one in the left. He repeated it.

Each man fell, spinning, as two balls from a Colt
Dragoon punched hot holes in them. Calhoun stood
with smoking pistols in hand, waiting to see if anyone
else was stupid enough to try to go against him. No
one was.

After glaring balefully at the few patrons who had
been unlucky enough to have been stuck in the wind-
whipped saloon, he uncocked the Dragoons and put
them away, one each in a cross-draw holster high up
on the front of his hipbones.

With something of a swagger, Calhoun strolled over
to one body. He bent and pulled his bowie knife free.
He wiped it on the man's shirt before sliding the long,
deadly knife into the sheath that dangled like a shoulder holster under his left arm. Still keeping a wary eye
out for possible danger, he scooped up his shabby
slouch hat and jammed it on his head.

Calhoun took two steps toward the door, then
stopped and turned back. Kneeling at the side of the
nearest body, he went through the man's pockets, taking out all the money he found—eight dollars and

twenty-nine cents, all in coins.

Standing, he tossed a silver dollar toward the frightened bartender. The coin hit the bar man on the chest and fell to the ground.

"That ought to cover what I drank," Calhoun growled.

He spun on the worn heel of his hide boots and strolled casually through the doors.

Once outside, he moved a little faster. He knew that someone would have gone for the sheriff—if the town had one—and the lawman would be coming soon enough. And even if the wretched town of Broken Wheel had no lawman, a posse would be sure to come after him before long.

He untied the reins of his horse from the hitching rail outside the saloon and pulled himself into the saddle. The animal he was riding these days was a bony, fragile-looking beast of indeterminate color and lineage.

The saddle was worth far more than the horse. It was of the finest saddle leather and had a large, Spanish saddle horn, about half the size of a dinner plate. The skirts and the *tapaderos*— Spanish-style stirrup covers—were hand-tooled with swirling figures. To each side of the saddlehorn was a holster encasing a large Colt Walker. On the right was a saddle scabbard holding a Henry percussion rifle; on the left was one in which rode a double-barreled 10-gauge shotgun loaded with buckshot.

Calhoun slapped the reins on the horse's rump and the animal began its bone-rattling trot up what passed for a street in Broken Wheel. By the time he was past the last building, the horse was lumbering along at a good clip. Calhoun gritted his teeth against the beast's ungainly gait.

Broken Wheel sat in Colorado Territory not far from the border with New Mexico Territory. Half a mile out of town, Calhoun stopped the horse and turned so he could look back toward Broken Wheel. A large cloud of dust rose in the distance, moving in his direction. The sound of hoofbeats was carried on the breeze.

"You boys are askin' for a heap of trouble," Calhoun said with quiet menace. He turned the horse and slapped it hard. The animal reluctantly lumbered off, galloping without enthusiasm, grace or much real speed.

He was angry because of the fracas. He usually was angry, but when such events occurred—which they did with disappointing regularity—Calhoun's rage built and boiled over.

Because of it, he viciously kept slapping the reins on the horse's rump. In his mind, he cursed the animal. And the Sioux who had disrupted his life several years ago. He hurled silent epithets at the workers on the Santa Fe Trail. And he spit oaths in his head at the town of Broken Wheel, and the residents of that festering sinkhole on the edge of nowhere.

While he was at it, he swore silently at the weather and the mountains and the rocks and chuckholes and anything else that flitted into his mind.

Despite the jolting ride, Calhoun occasionally glanced back over his shoulder. The cloud of dust never went away, but it didn't seem to be getting much closer either. It just followed along at the same distance.

The searing ball of sun beat down ferociously and the heat became unbearable. Even the normally constant breeze, the wind of the horse's struggling flight and the altitude didn't help cool things off much.

It was just another in a long line of irritations and troubles that plagued Wade Calhoun. Irritations and troubles that had started way back in Kansas Territory when he had left Lizbeth and Lottie on the farmstead to guide that wagon train. It was something the itchy-footed Calhoun did regularly.

But that time . . .

It was all his fault, he knew. The thought was something that never left him. The guilt hung over him like his own personal thundercloud.

CHAPTER

✳ 2 ✳

Calhoun did not slacken the horse's pace. He kept whipping the beast, getting every ounce of effort he could from the faltering animal.

He would hate to get caught out here in this vast, windswept open meadow dotted with aspen and pine. He figured that if he could find some cover, he would stop and make a stand. Those fools from back in Broken Wheel would be no match for a man who was well-armed, a deadly shot, and who cared little if he lived or died.

Mean-tempered Wade Calhoun met all those conditions, and then some.

But the countryside around here offered no place for him to hole up. So he continued to lash the horse on ruthlessly.

He finally entered some foothills that built quickly to a long, rugged slope leading toward the northern end of Raton Pass. The pass was still some miles south, but Calhoun turned the horse in that direction. He eased up on the animal just a bit, hoping the horse would be able to make it.

Another glance backward after some minutes of riding told him that the cloud of dust was still moving slowly but inexorably toward him. And gaining.

"Damn it all," Calhoun said as he whipped the rapidly weakening horse into a run once more. He thought the posse would have given up any hope of catching him a couple hours ago. Most posses from places like Broken Wheel were not this persistent. He knew that from experience.

He finally made it to the bulging, rocky knob and the horse wheezed as it bucked and jerked up the rough, slick-rock slope toward a pile of boulders and windswept pines.

The horse went to its front knees once, shoved up, and whinnied feebly. It moved on again, struggling mightily. It fell again and fought to regain its stance, but it couldn't.

"Hell, you've done as well as could be expected of an old bag of bones like you," Calhoun mumbled as he slipped out of the saddle. Actually, the horse had shown considerably more heart than Calhoun had given him credit for.

"Hold still, dammit," Calhoun snapped as he tried to unsaddle the still struggling horse.

He managed to get the cinch loosened and tugged off the saddle, blanket, saddlebags and bedroll. Calhoun could hear the posse's horses clacking on the stones already. He estimated they were less than half a mile behind.

He scrambled toward the rocks and trees a few yards up the scrubby slope. He dragged his gear with him, leaving the horse where it was.

As he settled into his rough fortress, Calhoun fleetingly thought it would be the kind thing to do to put a bullet through the horse's head. The horse had served him well enough and deserved a less painful ending than it was getting.

But Calhoun did not want to waste the powder and ball for the job. He might be fighting for his own life in a few minutes. He watched as the animal, without the weight of the rider and saddle, gawkily managed to get to its hooves. It stood there quivering feebly. Its ribby sides bellowed in and out.

Calhoun began checking his weapons. Unlike his horse and his appearance, they were of the finest quality. And all were well cared for. After all, they—and his innate ability to survive—were the only things that kept him alive for all these years.

Calhoun pulled out the two Walkers. The pistols weighed nearly five pounds apiece and had nine-inch-long barrels. They were accurate up to a hundred yards or so. They were good, powerful weapons, though they needed to be treated with care. He checked the five charges he kept in the six-shooters, then set them on a boulder in front of him.

He pulled the Henry rifle from the saddle scabbard and checked that, too. He contemplated also bringing out the shotgun, in case the posse got near enough for some close-in fighting. But he figured that they would not make it that close.

And if they did, the shotgun was near enough to hand, and he still had his backup weapon, a Walker with the barrel cut down to two inches. The pistol was loaded with fifty-seven grains of black powder, an awesomely heavy load. There was so much powder in each cylinder that a ball would barely fit. At close range, it was a devastating weapon.

Calhoun pulled off his worn, mousey-colored hat, exposing his matted hair. He wiped the sleeve of his soiled linsey-woolsey shirt across his sweaty forehead. It did not help cool him much. Neither did the several gulps of water he took from his wood canteen. He would have to be sparing in his use of water. The canteen was less than half full.

He raised the rifle, rested it across a rounded boulder, and took aim as he heard the horses approaching.

Nearly a dozen riders rode into view, and stopped when they saw Calhoun's horse. The animal seemed to have gained a little strength and was complacently—if still weakly—cropping the sparse grass between the rocks.

"We've got him afoot now, boys," a fat, slovenly, mustachioed man snapped arrogantly. The tin star on his chest glittered dully in the sunlight. He stopped next to Calhoun's horse. "He won't get far."

Calhoun fired the Henry. When the smoke cleared, the posse men and their mounts had disappeared. The sheriff was lying in a heap amid the talus and the prickly pear cactus.

Calhoun waited. He could hear some of the posse's horses galloping down the rocky trail. But through the puff of blue gunsmoke, he had dimly seen some figures slip off their horses and jump for the cover of rocks and pine trees. He figured several of the more timid posse men had fled, but there were always a few such men—foolish braggarts, mostly—in any group.

While he waited, Calhoun reloaded the rifle, taking his time. It was an arduous process, but he did it with practiced smoothness and care. First he poured powder down the barrel and then rammed a patched ball down with the ramrod. He slid a percussion cap over the nipple, and set the rifle down on half cock.

"Surrender, mister!" someone shouted.

Calhoun said nothing. He just watched and waited. He knew the posse would try something sooner or later, once the men had worked up their courage.

He did not have long to wait. He snatched up the two big Walkers and ducked behind the rough rock as he heard someone down in the rocks shout, "Now!"

As he had suspected, the men set up a fusillade.

Keeping his head down, Calhoun duck-walked a few feet to his right and cautiously peered around the biggest boulder of those that sheltered him.

Three posse men were running, crouched over. They skittered from rock to rock, from batch of cactus to pine tree.

He thumbed back the hammer of the Walker he held in his right hand and fired it twice.

Two of the running men went down. One did not move or make a sound. The other howled as he clutched his bloody leg.

"Damn," Calhoun mumbled. He was angry at himself, knowing he should have killed both. Well, he thought, it was too late to worry about that now. The man who was down would not be causing any trouble—or going anywhere. Calhoun figured he could pick the man off at leisure, should that become necessary.

"You all best haul your butts out of here, or I'll plant each and every goddamn one of you," Calhoun shouted. His voice was raspy from excitement, anger, and thirst. He was a man sparing in his speech, and that many words in one burst was unusual for him.

There was silence except for the hushed whisperings of the men out there and the steady groaning of the wounded man. Calhoun let them have their time to talk.

"I ain't gonna wait all goddamn day," he warned after a short interval.

"We'll head out," a man shouted. "But we'd like to take our dead and wounded with us."

"Fetch 'em. But y'all come out slow and easy."

Two men tentatively moved out from behind boulders. Both were unarmed, and each held his hands above his head. They had the look of men who were certain that they would be shot down by this madman at any instant.

Calhoun squatted in his shelter, Walkers in hand, watching tensely.

The two men helped their wounded companion up. Just as they did, a mounted posse man returned with a few runaway horses.

Aided by his two friends, the wounded man limped to a horse. He allowed his friends to help him into the saddle. Then the two threw the bodies of the sheriff and the other posse man across the saddle of one mount. One man then climbed up behind the wounded man.

In minutes, all the other posse men had warily come out from their hiding places and pulled themselves quickly into saddles. Most had to double up since so many horses had run off.

Calhoun considered ordering the posse to leave one behind for him. But most were already riding double. Besides, his own horse seemed to have recovered.

The posse galloped away, each man half-expecting

to receive a farewell bullet in the back.

Calhoun watched them ride off. When they were gone, he walked up to his horse. And swore. From a distance—even a short one—the horse had looked to be fine. But now Calhoun could see that the animal was broken. Calhoun knew he could not ride the horse a mile. Without emotion, he fired the Walker, putting a ball through the animal's head. Then he walked back to his haven. He sat back to wait, just in case some of the posse men had decided to stay behind.

Calhoun contemplated his immediate future. He was miles from anywhere with no horse, almost no food and only half a canteen of water. His prospects were not bright.

Calhoun sat on a rock, rolled a cigarette, and fired it up. He sat, thinking. But the decision was easy. The only place he could reasonably expect to find help would be down in New Mexico Territory. With places like Taos, Santa Fe and Las Vegas within a couple weeks' walk, he felt he had a fighting chance of making it.

Once in a town like one of those, he would do whatever it took to get a stake. He was not above some illegal enterprise on occasion to fill his pocket when the need was there.

But more attractive to him was the knowledge that there would be opportunities for honest and mostly respectable work in those places. The Army could always use good scouts and he considered himself one of the best. There were freight trains along the Santa Fe Trail and wagon trains heading toward California that could use his services.

Calhoun waited two hours, taking the time to clean the weapons he had used. He did them one at a time, keeping the others ready.

Then he climbed a steep cliff and stood precariously on a small, rocky ledge. Shading his eyes with hat and hand, he stared out into the sunbaked expanse of meadow that ran away from the mountain to the north. He could see the cloud of dust from the posse some miles away. He nodded.

Scrambling back down, he gathered some pine wood and made a small fire. While he waited for the coffee to brew, he butchered some of the meat from the horse. He had no hankering for horse meat, but with only a small sack of beans and a few bits of bacon and salted beef, he could not be choosy.

He cooked some of the horse meat. Without expression, he choked it down. He needed the nourishment; the taste did not matter.

He spent the rest of the day and that night in the same spot. Using a small, slow fire and its attendant smoke, he jerked as much of the horse meat as he thought he could carry with him.

After another meal of horse meat in the morning, he packed his jerky and coffeepot in his saddlebags. Hefting the weighty saddle over his left shoulder, he moved toward a small cleft that would bring him to Raton Pass—and thus into New Mexico Territory.

He shuffled along, heading slowly up the long, swelling slope toward Raton Pass. As he walked he though about the fracas in Broken Wheel.

CHAPTER

⋆ 3 ⋆

Calhoun was not a man easily bothered by violence such as that he had encountered in Broken Wheel. But he had a tendency—when he had time to review such things—of trying to make sure what he had done was right by his lights. It was all that mattered. If he stayed true to himself, he was satisfied.

He had entered Broken Wheel almost out of money and short of prospects. Like usual. He had moseyed on down from the high mountains of Colorado Territory, figuring that he could find work along the mountain branch of the Santa Fe Trail. If not there, then certainly in Cimarron or Taos, Las Vegas or one of the other cities in northern New Mexico Territory.

Calhoun had been in these parts before, but he had never seen Broken Wheel before. Like so many other places in the violent, wild place called the West, it apparently had sprung up out of nothing overnight.

Broken Wheel was a town that had a rough, unfinished look. Construction was going on all over, and what streets there were sprawled haphazardly all over. Houses—most of them little more than crude shacks—spread out across the high, rolling plains.

Most of the businesses operated out of tents; others in shacks poorly made of wood or tin sheeting.

Only a few were in substantial wood and adobe structures.

The wind blew almost continuously off the mountains to the west and southwest. It whipped at the grungy little town in fits and starts, snapping the canvas of the tents and threatening the precarious wood buildings.

Despite the desolate poorness of the place, people hustled every which way; horses and carriages and wagons rode recklessly up and down streets made muddy by the recent rains. Occasional gunfire could be heard, as well as the continuous din of saloons, gambling halls and bawdyhouses.

Calhoun ran a practiced eye over Broken Wheel as he rode in. He had seen dozens, scores maybe, of towns just like it. They had little to offer. But for a fleeting few moments, a saddle tramp such as himself could sate his baser appetites. He judged that the place had started when someone had broken a wagon wheel while traveling on the Santa Fe Trail. That would have given the place its name—and its only reason for existence.

But none of that really mattered to Calhoun. It had saloons, restaurants and bawdyhouses. He spotted what was supposed to be a mercantile store and shrugged. He could use some supplies, but his pocket cash was perilously low.

Calhoun stopped at the first saloon he spotted. It was a large tent with a simple sign whose paint had been sanblasted almost into oblivion. It said simply:

WHISKEY

WOMEN

FOOD

Calhoun figured it would do. He stopped before a

hitching rail and dismounted. After tying the horse to the post, he glanced around. No one was paying him any heed. He reached into the pocket of his worn wool pants and pulled out his supply of money and counted it. He had the grand total of six dollars and fifty-two cents.

He spat in disgust. Such a fortune would not get him far. On the other hand, he needed work anyway and was confident he would find something soon. If not, there were other ways to put a little cash in his pockets.

He decided that spending his six dollars and change on a spree wouldn't be such a bad thing. It wouldn't be much of a spree, either. He would do what he could with what he had.

The open maw of the shabby tent saloon beckoned, and he gave in to the seduction of it. Tables were scattered about, each with a smelly, smoky, coal-oil lantern burning on it. The light helped dispel some of the gloom that was little relieved by the grayness of the cloudy day.

He wandered to the bar—several barely planed planks resting on four massive kegs—two at each end. "Whiskey," he growled at the surly bartender.

"Glass or bottle?"

"Bottle."

"Two dollars. Pay now."

Calhoun stared at the rancid-looking man for a moment. Then he slapped two silver dollars down on the planks.

The bartender scooped them up and the coins disappeared. The bar man turned and then spun back, a bottle in his hand. He thunked it down on the bar, followed by a dirty glass. Then he slumped off down the bar, only partly aware that Calhoun's hot eyes were boring on his back.

Calhoun pulled the cork from the bottle and dropped it. He picked the bottle up and sniffed at the small opening. The whiskey's bouquet reminded the saddle tramp of a small barn with too many horses that had recently drank more than their fill of water.

He shrugged. He had drunk some pretty poor stuff at times. He figured this couldn't be much worse than some of them. He filled the shot glass, set the bottle down, and jolted the shot down his throat.

And gagged.

He had been wrong. This was the worst panther piss he had ever had. And it was watered down considerably, besides. He didn't know what angered him more.

Calhoun spit a few times, trying to rid his mouth of the foul aftertaste.

"Somethin' wrong?" the bartender asked innocently, wandering back up.

Calhoun glared at the bartender a moment, assessing the man. The barkeep was big but carrying a considerable amount of fat. Calhoun could see that the bartender thought he was a hardcase, but Calhoun knew better. He might be able to awe the damnfool residents of Broken Wheel, but he made little impression on Calhoun.

"Give me a different bottle," Calhoun answered coldly. "One that ain't come straight from a sick cow."

"You sayin' there's somethin' wrong with my whiskey?" the bartender asked, offended.

"Yep."

"I don't take kindly to such insinuations," the bartender said in a voice that usually had men quaking with its menace. He placed his hands flat on the bar and leaned forward a little.

Calhoun was still unimpressed. He glared into the bartender's eyes. Suddenly the bowie knife was in his hand and he jabbed it deep into the planks. Though he had not taken his eyes from the bartender's, the knife imbedded itself in the wood in the half an inch of space between the man's thumb and forefinger.

The belligerence fled from the bartender's eyes. He glanced down at the still-quivering knife and eased his hand away. He grabbed the offending bottle and pulled it back. "Must've been a bad batch or sumpin," he muttered.

The bartender turned and set the bottle down on a crate. He moved away and rummaged in another wooden box and came out with a different bottle. He set that down before Calhoun and stepped back, waiting anxiously.

Calhoun pulled the cork, then filled the shot glass. With only a moment's hesitation—to let the bartender sweat—Calhoun dumped the contents of the glass down his throat. He swallowed.

"Ahhh," he said, drawing the word out. He very gently set the glass on the bar. "Better."

The bartender smiled in relief. Calhoun did not return the grin. The bartender wandered away, both relieved and worried.

Calhoun poured another drink. He let it sit there while he rolled and lighted a smoke. He was as content as he could get. He turned and rested his elbows on the plank bar, watching the other patrons. His eyes moved from one man to the next, as he assessed each. None appeared to be a threat to him.

Half an hour later, a voice next to him said, "Buy a girl a drink, mister?"

He half-turned and looked at the person possessing the voice. She was short and quite chubby. Mousy hair was sprawled in tangles over her head and dropped over her sloping forehead. Dull eyes looked at him expectantly. An overly long jaw supported a mouth with a serious underbite. She was rather repugnant looking.

Calhoun was about to tell her to get lost, but he figured she was just trying to make her way through life as best as she could. Just like he was. He had the bartender bring another glass, and he poured her a drink. Calhoun figured there was no harm in that. He would give her a few drinks and tell her to be on her way.

The woman gratefully picked up the drink and slurped half of it down. While she did that, Calhoun looked around the saloon. He quickly came to the numbing conclusion that as repulsive as this woman might be, she was perhaps the most attractive of the fallen angels who were trying to ply their trade in the foul saloon. He knew from experience that Broken Wheel, being as it was on the edge of nowhere, could not attract many of the finer women in that profession.

"Another?" the woman asked hopefully.

Calhoun complied.

She left it sitting on the bar as she stared up at him. Sweat glistened on her upper lip. Her eyes seemed not to focus very well. "You interested?" she asked, her voice flat.

"I reckon," Calhoun allowed. "How much?"

"Two bucks."

Calhoun grunted an affirmative.

"Name's Round Bess," the woman said as she lifted her glass.

"Wade." It was all she needed to know, he figured.

Round Bess knew better than to ask for more. Such questions were not asked in a place like Broken Wheel. She did not know if Wade was really the man's name. Nor did she much care. Her name was not Bess. They were not here to get married and settle down. She poured the drink down. "Well, come on then, big man," she said with a wisp of a weary smile.

"You mind my bottle?" he said to the bartender. His tone made it clear that the bartender would forfeit his life if anything happened to the bottle while Calhoun was gone.

"Yessir."

Calhoun let himself be led away. There was a slit opening in the back of the saloon tent, and they went through that. Outside, there were five small tents. Round Bess led him to one. Its only furnishings were a cot with a thin blanket, a small table on which a pitcher and basin sat, and one fragile chair.

Round Bess turned to face him, loosening the bodice of her thin cotton dress as she did.

Not long afterward, Calhoun was standing at the bar again, puffing on a cigarette and nursing another drink. He had noticed that in the short time he was gone, several more men had entered the saloon. One group of seven men sat at a table. He thought they might bear watching.

Within minutes, Round Bess was at that table. Two of the men began pawing at her. The plump little woman tried to dodge some of the more offensive grabbing but had only a little success. Her initial smiles quickly turned to heated retorts.

Calhoun let it go on for a while. He usually did not get involved in the problems of other folks. But he was not the kind of man to stand by and watch a woman being abused. Not even a fallen angel. She had a right to whatever dignity she could muster.

When one of the men—a good-size fellow with a scar down one cheek—slapped Round Bess, Calhoun had had enough. "Watch the bottle again," he said to the bartender.

Calhoun strode to the table. Round Bess had her back to him. One of the men at the table had his arm around her, preventing her from leaving. Calhoun peeled the man's arm away, surprising him.

"These boys bought your time, ma'am?" Calhoun asked.

"No," Round Bess said, relieved.

Calhoun took his last two dollars from his pocket and put them in Bess's hand. "Then I am. Come." He tugged her away.

"Hey, dammit," the big man at the table shouted.

Calhoun turned and fixed deadly eyes on the man. "Yes?" he asked, voice hard.

"We was about to . . ." the man started.

"Well, I did." Calhoun turned and stalked away, towing Bess after him.

They spent more time than was necessary in the tent crib out back. Bess was afraid of the men at the table, and Calhoun could see no reason to rush her back into the saloon.

Finally she said, "Please tell Mulrooney, the bartender, that I took sick, would you?" she implored.

Calhoun nodded and left. He told the bartender. He had just filled his glass again when the man whose arm Calhoun had unpeeled from around Bess slammed him in the back.

Calhoun grunted from the blow. But he jerked an arm sharply backward. His elbow caught the man in the face. The man fell back a step. Calhoun whirled, his bowie knife in his right hand. With his left, he grabbed the man's soiled shirt and pulled. That was when the bowie knife bit deep into the man's fat stomach and all hell broke loose.

CHAPTER

* 4 *

As Calhoun settled down for the night, he concluded that he had acted properly by his own lights. He often was the source of his own troubles, he knew, but this time, at least, he was innocent of causing trouble. He had simply defended a woman's honor. It made no difference what kind of woman she was. She was a woman, and that was good enough for him. She did not deserve to be pummeled by a table full of damn fools.

And he had defended his own life. There was nothing wrong with such a thing. Anyone would agree with that. He had done nothing more than was required of him. He began building a little fire, satisfied with himself.

Some of the satisfaction dwindled as he pulled out his supply of jerked horse meat. He looked at it with distaste. He had nothing much else, so it would have to do.

Calhoun poured enough water into his coffeepot for one good-size cup of coffee. Then he set the pot near the flames. He shook the canteen and shrugged once more. What the hell, he figured. He poured almost all the rest into a small pot he had. Then he added the last of his beans and set that pot to cooking.

He smoked a cigarette while he waited for his dinner to cook. When it was hot, he ate and drank slowly. There was little to savor about the supper. But it might be the last decent meal he would have in some time, so he tried to enjoy it as much as he could.

Tired, he climbed into his bedroll just after he finished eating. For just a moment, he wondered again at all the troubles he had encountered in the past few years. He wondered if it were all his fault somehow. Then the blessed peace of sleep overcame him.

Calhoun poured the last of his water into his coffeepot the next morning. He enjoyed the thick, pungent Arbuckle's, drinking half of it down right off. Then he choked down a few pieces of horse meat jerky. He finished the coffee—quickly reheated—as he smoked a cigarette.

He almost smiled as he thought of his predicament. He had been in positions as bad as this one before. He figured that once he got through the pass, he would be able to find some game. It might take another day or two of traveling, since he was on foot. But he could live that long on the horse meat jerky he had left.

Water, however, could become a problem. He felt certain that he would be able to find a creek or spring or even a mud puddle sooner or later. He had better, or he'd not last a couple of days. Still, he would worry about that when the time came.

Within minutes he had packed his meager supplies. He made water into the fire, and then kicked dirt and stones over the mess. Hoisting the heavy saddle, he strode off. By midmorning he had picked up the Santa

Fe Trail. It wasn't so much of a road here as it was a series of ruts in the muddy soil. But they were easy to follow.

The land began to rise steadily, and the ground became more rocky. Combined with the ruts, mud, dust and other aberrations of the land, it made the going tough.

By noon, Calhoun was drenched in sweat and laboring. He stopped and looked around. He decided that he was almost halfway up the northern side of the pass. He had a hell of a way to go yet, he thought sourly, before traveling would get any easier.

He paused there only long enough to gnaw down two strips of horse meat. His tongue felt swollen, and he regretted having wasted some water last night making beans. He wished he had that water now. Not only did he need it, the liquid would also make swallowing the horse meat a little easier.

Calhoun picked up a couple of pebbles and popped them in his mouth. They would help keep him producing saliva. At least for a while. Once more he hefted the saddle—which seemed to have gained about four hundred pounds in the past half day—and marched on.

As night drifted over him, he stopped again. He ate a little more jerky, and began spreading out his bedroll. Suddenly he stopped and snarled softly, "Hell." The word sounded odd, coming out of his dry mouth, partially blocked by his thirst-swollen tongue.

He rolled up the blankets again and tied them behind the saddle. Then he lifted the saddle and walked on. He moved slowly. The rocky, undulating ground was treacherous in the dark. But the temperature was down, and a fine mist seemed to cling to the air. It eased his insufferable thirst minutely.

Dawn found Calhoun stumbling forward on rapidly weakening legs. He would stop, stand there weaving a few moments and then lurch on, like a drunk trying to walk in an earthquake. He could no longer raise a spit. His eyes were bleary and he had trouble seeing, even after the sun had broken over the rim of the horizon.

Worse, his mind was playing tricks on him. He saw people he had known who were long dead. He saw places hundreds of miles away suddenly transplanted in front of him. He envisioned dinner tables sagging with the weight of buffalo steaks and elk roasts and hams and other foodstuffs.

He tripped and fell. His reactions, honed by years of gunfights, fist fights and other dangers, allowed him to catch himself before his face smacked on the ground. But the jolt of his right knee landing on a rough-edged rock snapped him out of his mental wanderings.

Leaving his saddle on the ground, Calhoun pushed himself up. He tested his right leg. The knee was a little painful, but was not really damaged. He looked around. He was rather surprised to see that the trail of wagon ruts still stretched out before him. He had managed to keep to the road despite the darkness and his inattention.

He turned slowly to his left, squinting against the day's new sun. He kept turning and then stopped. He could see the summit of the pass back there. He had made it.

Calhoun continued his circle. Off to the west, he saw a grove of aspens. Brush was thick between the trees, and Calhoun thought he could hear water bubbling. He wondered if there were really a creek or whether it was all his imagination again. He became aware of the thick mucus in his mouth. What he would give for a full canteen right now!

He had to find out. He grabbed the saddle and lifted it. The saddle felt like it weighed more than the horse he had taken it from. But he marched forward on legs wobbly from the lack of food and water.

Calhoun crashed into the brush and through it, as if pulled by the sound of running water. He had to get there. Branches and brambles tore at his clothes and flesh, but he felt none of it.

Suddenly he was almost knee-deep in a fast-rushing creek of icy water. He did not care right now if this was an illusion. It was real enough to him. He sank to his knees, reveling in the cold rush of water. Still holding onto the saddle, he bent at the waist, resting on his right hand in the water. He plunged his face into the water. He drank and drank, gulping down water as if he would never get enough of it.

Finally he came up for air. He snapped his head back and forth, splattering water all around. He whooped twice, the sound eerily ricocheting off the Sangre de Cristo Mountains.

"Damn!" he muttered. He drank a little more. But he was sated, especially knowing that water was near at hand and would remain so for as long as he wanted it.

He stood and moved to the riverbank. Though he was still weak, he felt strength returning. He dropped the dripping saddle. Now that sense and reason had returned, he became his usual, proficient, calculating self again. The first thing he did was to check all his weapons.

The Colt Dragoons were still dry, but the Walkers, the Henry and the shotgun were damp. He cleaned, oiled and reloaded each one and then rested them on the dry earth rather than placing them back in the saddle scabbards.

As he sat in the dappled shadows working on his weapons, he spotted an otter poking its head curiously from the water. He snapped off a shot, nodding with satisfaction when he hit the otter.

After finishing cleaning his guns, he skinned and gutted the otter. Then he built up a fire, put on coffee, and dangled the otter carcass over the fire from a green stick.

In a short time he was gulping down coffee and chewing down bolts of half-raw otter. It tasted little better than the horse meat, but it was fresh. That was enough for now.

He spent three days in the comfortable spot alongside the unnamed creek. He used the time to regain his strength. The night he arrived, he brought down a deer. That kept him in fresh meat.

Two days later, he shot another deer. He jerked the meat over slow fires. As a final act of defiance, he tossed the remaining pieces of his horse meat jerky into the creek. Calhoun felt no regret about it as he watched the foul-tasting meat being swept away by the swift water.

He seemed to be unable to get his fill of water. Calhoun walked around the campsite for those three days with a perpetual feeling of being bloated. But still he made regular trips—almost pilgrimages—to the creek and tried to drain it.

Soon he was ready to leave. He never was one for sitting in one place too long. It was the main reason he had taken to scouting in the first place. And it was why he was filled with guilt. If only he could stay put a while. . .

Calhoun angrily shoved the thought away. People were what they were. He had found that out long ago. There was no changing it. He lifted the saddle with practiced ease. With renewed spirit, he strode off, his long, strong legs moving at a deceptively ground-eating pace.

He slowed soon, though. For one thing, he knew that he could not keep up that pace for long. For another, he wasn't in all that much of a hurry. And, most importantly, the road, such as it was, now headed into the mountains. The road rolled up one hill and down into a valley, then back up. A meadow came along now and then, offering some flat, easy travel.

Calhoun took it all in stride. Each hill or canyon, cliff or forest was just another obstacle to be conquered and Calhoun considered himself a conqueror. He had long ago determined that nothing would defeat him. At least not without one hell of a fight first.

He made good progress, not bothering to stop more than briefly at the noon hour for a hasty meal. When it got too dark to see well, Calhoun would stop wherever it was convenient and make his small campsite.

The pattern followed day in, day out for more than a week. The countryside varied little, and his routine not at all. Boredom began to set in.

CHAPTER

* 5 *

Calhoun had nowhere to hide and nowhere to run when the three men charged at him on horseback. He was trudging across an open meadow maybe a mile long and half that wide.

He was three-quarters across it when the three horsemen bolted out from the pines ahead of him. They bore down on him rapidly.

Calhoun took two seconds to assess the situation. It was not good, that much was evident. But it could be worse.

He dropped the saddle and pulled the Henry rifle. His practiced eye saw that it was ready. He knelt and brought the rifle up to his shoulder. Calhoun waited, aiming. He knew that he would get only one shot with the rifle, and wanted to be absolutely certain his shot was true.

He fired.

As the wind tore away the powder smoke from in front of his face, he saw two mounted men and one riderless horse galloping toward him. In the distance, he spotted a man bouncing on the ground. He nodded.

"Goddamn fools," he muttered as he placed the rifle down on the ground at his side. He pulled one of the two Walkers from the saddle holsters. They were bigger, heavier, and had a longer range than the Dragoons.

Bullets kicked up small clots of earth around him. But Calhoun calmly stood his ground. He still had nowhere to run and he knew that two men riding as recklessly as these two would have a devil of a time hitting anything. He waited patiently, unflinching as more balls struck all around. Most fell far short, being fired as they were from pistols.

"Just a little closer," Calhoun whispered. Suddenly his hat flew off, carried away by a bullet. He smiled humorlessly.

Still kneeling on one knee, Calhoun brought the Walker up in his right hand. His left hand braced the right wrist.

The two riders split, planning to sweep to each side of him. It was a wise move, and what Calhoun would have done. But he was not worried by it.

He fired the Walker twice. Without waiting to see whether he had hit anything, Calhoun swung. He brought the Walker to bear on the third attacker. He felt a ball tug at his shirt, but he managed not to flinch.

He fired twice more. He flopped onto his stomach, dropping the Walker at his side. He rolled several times, grabbing the second Walker from the saddle holster along the way. He stopped and waited, listening. He could hear the horses still running. But the enemy gunfire had stopped.

Calhoun peered through the grass. He could see two riderless horses trotting away. Glancing off his shoulder, he saw the third. It, too, had no rider.

He stayed put, waiting. The sun's heat beat down

on his bare head. Calhoun tensed, thumbing back the revolver's hammer, as a five-foot-long rattlesnake slithered by a few feet in front of him. That and a hawk screeching far above were the only signs of life.

Until buzzards began gathering overhead. The big, ugly birds circled lazily in the cloudless sky. Calhoun figured then that all three men who had charged him were dead.

He rose cautiously, into a half-crouch. He circled, pistol still at the ready. But no gunfire came. He eased the hammer of the Walker down and jammed the weapon into the saddle holster. He pulled one of his Dragoons and headed off toward the southwest.

He found all three men. Two were dead, flies buzzing around the bloody bullet holes in their torsos. The third was alive, but in agony. Calhoun's ball had punctured the man's gut, and he would linger a while in exquisite agony before dying, too.

"Want me to end it for you?" Calhoun asked non-committally.

"Go to hell," the man gasped. His face screwed up as he tried to keep in the screams that wanted release.

"Suit yourself." Calhoun spun and walked away, leaving the man moaning in the dirt. He walked back to his saddle. There he cleaned the Walkers and reloaded them.

He watched all around him as he worked. Two of the attackers' horses were long gone. But the third was less than three hundred yards away. Calhoun worked slowly, methodically, hoping that the horse would grow used to him and move closer.

By the time he had finished the pistols and reloaded the rifle, the horse had showed no signs of moving toward its former master. Indeed, it seemed to be more skittish. That was understandable, considering the growing number of buzzards, wolves, and coyotes showing up.

Calhoun wanted that horse. And he figured he had only one chance to get it. What he was about to try seldom worked. But he could see no other choice.

He raised the Henry rifle once more and aimed. Then he fired. The horse took three giant leaps before collapsing. "Shit," Calhoun shouted. A profound silence held for some moments. Then nature's sounds returned.

Calhoun reloaded the rifle one more time. He carried it in his left hand as he walked slowly toward the horse. The animal was on its side, hooves kicking erratically. Calhoun shook his head.

He had wanted to wing the horse across the neck, which would stun it for a little while. But either Calhoun had flinched or the horse had moved. The bullet had sunk deep into the horse's neck. The animal was not dead, but it was paralyzed, and would never be any good to anyone.

With a note of sadness—at his lack of success, not at the horse's imminent demise—Calhoun slid the bowie knife out. He drew it swiftly, and surely along the underside of the horse's neck, slitting its throat.

When the horse stopped kicking, Calhoun went through the saddlebags. He found a sack of Arbuckle's coffee and some bacon wrapped in oiled paper. It wasn't much, but it would stretch Calhoun's meager larder some.

He returned to his saddle and put the foodstuffs in his own saddlebags. He was almost glad he had not found more food. He had little room left in his saddlebags, and he wasn't sure he could lug around much more.

He shrugged and shoved the Henry into the scabbard. Then he lugged his saddle off as he revisited each man he had shot. He went through the pockets of all three. The one was still living.

"One more chance to die in peace," Calhoun offered.

But the man was beside himself in agony. He just moaned incoherently. Calhoun shrugged, pocketed the three dollars he had found on the man and walked off.

At one of the bodies, Calhoun had to kill two wolves before he could go through the man's pockets. Killing the wolves sent the rest of the pack backing off, snarling, and the buzzards flapped away heavily.

Once back at his saddle, Calhoun counted up his take. He had brought in fifteen dollars and fifteen cents. With the little bit of his own money and that he had taken in Broken Wheel, he had just under twenty-three dollars.

It was a veritable fortune compared with what he had had when he had arrived in Broken Wheel. But certainly not enough to get him anywhere. Hell, he thought disgustedly, it wasn't even enough to buy him a broken down nag of a horse.

Still, it was better than being bitten by a snake, he figured. He considered for a moment having a meal here. But the presence of so many scavengers would make a meal uncomfortable.

Grabbing his expensive, steadily heavier saddle, he walked off. As he walked past the gut-shot man, he shook his head at the man's stupidity. Had it been him lying there with the fire in his belly like that, he would've been happy to accept the relief of a bullet to the brain. But each to his own, he figured.

He made the cool comfort of the pines, and soon after decided he was far enough away from the carnage to be left in peace. He pulled up, made a small fire, and ate all the bacon he had taken from the saddlebags.

The bacon was half a step from being rancid, but Calhoun relished its fattiness. It seemed to thicken his blood and give him immediate strength.

Once more he kept on the move, struggling up rocky hills, sliding down the other side of them. He splashed across shallow creeks and clambered over rocky promontories, trying to save a little time by taking shortcuts.

Night found him in a barren spot of rocks and boulders. There was no water, but his canteen was full. There was no wood for a cookfire, but he needed no fire for his venison jerky.

Something woke him from a deep sleep. He lay, scarcely breathing, trying to decipher what it was. Then came an almost imperceptible padding. Calhoun blinked. Now that he knew what it was, he could formulate a plan and take action.

He had been using his saddle as something of a pillow. He reached up and grabbed one of the Walkers and waited, listening to the quiet pacing a few feet off.

Calhoun figured the big mountain cat was waiting to make sure of his prey. The man scent would keep the animal at bay for a little while. But Calhoun knew it would not do so for too long.

Suddenly Calhoun rolled out of the blankets, snapping the revolver up. He fired all five shots as fast as he could, tracking the cat through the dim light cast by the moon. The mountain lion had whirled and raced off at the suddenness and unexpectedness of the saddle tramp's initial movement.

The cougar jerked as each bullet punched into its innards. By the time the fifth hit it, the cat could barely move. Still, the animal moved instinctively, crawling across the rocks, seeking its hidden lair.

Calhoun dropped the Walker on his blankets. He rose, pulling out a Dragoon. He moved cautiously toward the cougar. But the animal was dead. Calhoun felt a momentary sadness. The mountain lion was, he thought, a courageous animal. One that lived and died by its wits. Much like himself. And while he could muster no compassion for the death of men who lived vaingloriously—like those who had attacked him earlier in the day—he could find just a spark of sympathy for such a noble animal as this one.

The feeling was fleeting. Within minutes, he was curled up in his robes again, snoring peacefully.

During the next week of traveling, Calhoun began to see a few scattered signs of life. He occasionally caught glimpses of men riding, and once, he spotted a wagon. He considered trying to get a ride from the man on the wagon, but he was too embarrassed. He salved his conscience by telling himself he would never have been able to catch up to it on foot anyway.

But as he traveled, he began to consider the possibilities. He finally settled on Cimarron. The town was on the branch of the Santa Fe Trail that broke off, crossed the Sangre de Cristos and wound its way to Taos.

Cimarron was the nearest city of any size that he knew about. He was sure he would be able to find scouting or guiding work there. Or at least hear of where he could find such work.

With a destination set in mind and the possibility of reaching it relatively soon, Calhoun began moving a little faster. His steps were sure and strong. He had not wanted for water of late, almost always finding a spring or creek where he could camp.

He had always been an excellent hunter, and that skill proved its worth many times over. Deer, elk, and mountain sheep all fell to the Henry rifle.

The venison jerky became almost a memory to him. He used it only as something to nibble on or gnaw while he was walking. He had fresh meat just about every day.

Calhoun continued to avoid contact with people, though. He wasn't sure why, but he figured he would wait until he got to Cimarron before he would talk with anyone. Not that he had seen all that many people, even lately.

The land began rising sharply, and he knew he was getting close. It had been a few years since he had been to Cimarron, and he looked forward to getting there.

CHAPTER

* 6 *

Calhoun limped into Cimarron a week later. He was in the poorest of humors. The last week had been hellacious.

The trail he had to follow had grown steadily steeper. The knee he had injured a while back began to bother him some as he had to put more and more strain on it.

His hide boots were worn through until it felt like he was walking on paper soles. A blister had popped up on his right heel and another on the ball of the same foot. Both had burst and were running. He had stepped on a prickly pair cactus and took a thorn in his left arch, leaving that foot sore, too.

His food had run out not long ago, so he had subsisted on whatever he could catch. He was a good hunter, but without a horse he was limited to what he could take with him. Besides, game grew more scarce the closer he got to town. The venison jerky has lasted a while, but even that had begun to run low.

By the time he reached Cimarron, he was out of coffee, flour. . . indeed, everything but a few paltry strips of the venison jerky and a full canteen.

Though he had slept well enough, he was still tired since he refused to stop before he had put in an eighteen hour day, each and every day. The long days afoot had wearied him, though he did not show it.

But those factors could not stop him from paying close attention to Cimarron as he trod slowly down what passed for the main street. The town had not changed much since he was here last.

Cimarron was a town that had a rough, though permanent look. Except for the large main thoroughfare—actually a segment of an offshoot of the Santa Fe Trail—what streets there were sprawled haphazardly all over. Cimarron had its share of rickety, tilting shacks, but quite a few of the houses and businesses were substantial buildings.

The place was hectic with activity. Children ran about, screeching in their games and excitement. Dogs yapped and barked in a raucous cacophony. Some chased their young masters; others snarled at each other over scraps of meat.

Heavy freight wagons rumbled up and down the main street as people scurried out of the way. Muleskinners shouted and swore at their animals, blistering the plodding beasts with language that was as blue as the skies over New Mexico Territory.

There were more civilized folk, too. Women and shopkeepers went about their business, either oblivious to the cursing, sweating teamsters, or ignoring them with practiced aplomb.

Despite these signs of refinement, Cimarron was still a rough town on the fringe of civilization, and as such, it attracted more than its share of hardcases, outlaws, and other malcontents. All of which meant that gunfire broke out with annoying frequency, starting over nothing and, more often than not, ending without too much bodily harm to anyone.

Wade Calhoun felt at home here. If he wasn't so tired, sore and irritable, he might have even cracked a smile.

Calhoun slowed his pace, stopping to lean against the wooden side of a hardware store. He rested his saddle in the dust at his feet and breathed in deeply. The pungent aroma of horse droppings mingled with the sharp spiciness of Mexican cooking. It was as near to heaven as he thought he would ever get. The smell of food quickly reminded him of how hungry he was.

There were numerous restaurants, saloons, and hotels, as well as other places that could be counted on to provide a meal. He wondered which one to choose. He had never found a way to make this decision easily. He finally decided to walk on a little more, to see if anything particularly struck his fancy.

He was alert and interested as he wandered aimlessly up the street. At each intersection, he would stop and look down the side street or alley. He had learned a long time ago that some of the best places were not on the main street of a town. It paid to look around some.

Just past the center of town, he spotted a familiar sign down a small side street that was almost an alley. The sign hung out over the street on a long iron rod so that folks passing by on the main street could read it easily. Big, bold letters in bright-red paint announced: MOTHER POWELL'S CHOP HOUSE

Calhoun did grin then. It was the first time a real grin had creased his hard features in years.

"I'll be damned," he whispered into the wind.

He turned down the alley. As he neared the sagging building, he noticed that under the chop house sign was another sign in fading paint. It said: Rooms available.

Calhoun nodded. It had to be Mother Powell's place. No one else could have a sign painted with those big, brassy letters in that bold, flowing hand. He could not believe his luck in finding Mother Agatha Powell in Cimarron, New Mexico Territory. The last he had heard, Mother Powell was off in California somewhere, catering to the miners in the gold fields of the Sierra Nevada.

Calhoun's spirits took a marked upturn. Help was near at hand. Even if work was not forthcoming, he knew that he would at least have food, and a roof over his head, until he could find a job and get back on his feet.

With his Scotch-Irish heritage, Calhoun was a proud man. Sometimes obstinately so. He was not a man who took—or gave—help lightly. Asking for it was almost beyond him. But Mother Agatha Powell was one person, perhaps the only one, he would not be afraid to ask for help. And he had no doubt whatsoever that he would receive it.

Mother Agatha Powell could not be considered a saint by any means. She was simply an adventuresome, open, friendly woman who was also kind and generous to a fault. Particularly to men and women who were downtrodden and who had faced some rough times. She was a friend to all and helped anyone in need.

Not many people knew that side of her. Most folks simply shook their heads at her seemingly eccentric and decidedly unladylike behavior. But those who needed her soon found out about her. God only knew how. They would end up at her door where she would offer them whatever help she could.

She had been raised, and started doing occasional good deeds for her neighbors, in the Appalachian Mountains. That was where she had met and married Ezra Powell. She had no qualms about leaving her family and friends and moving ever westward with Ezra. They had made their home for a while in Mississippi and Arkansas and Missouri and Kansas Territory.

Ezra Powell was a hard-working merchant and did well, though he never got rich. Still, he and his tall, broad-shouldered wife were well-off enough for him to be able to freely indulge Agatha's occasional displays of quiet beneficence. He grumbled about it if anyone was around, but privately, he was a proud as a gamecock at what Agatha did.

Eventually, Ezra had moved them to Texas, where he died at the hands of a war party of Comanches. Mother Powell, as she was called by virtually everyone even then, took stock of what she had and what she could do.

She was a widow in her early thirties, with a ten-year-old child. She was alone in a small town on the Texas frontier. She had a little cash that Ezra had put away, and the house in town, as well as the store Ezra had operated. She decided to stick it out a while. She was an excellent cook but a poor businesswoman. So she soon sold the general store and opened a restau-

rant. Later she began taking in boarders at her house,
until she ended up having to open a proper boarding
house. She did all right, though she sometimes gave
away more than she made.

Eventually, out of the goodness of her heart, she
began taking in strays, orphans and runaways mostly.
They were, almost without exception, misfit children
whom no one else wanted. She would tidy them up
and try to get them a little schooling. She would
apprentice the boys out, and teach household skills to
the girls. Then she would send them out into the
world to make their own way. Most did well; a few did
not.

Many of the folks in Flat Neck, Texas, did not like
her efforts. They began to talk about Mother Powell,
whispering that the kindly, attractive woman was really running a brothel with the girls she took in and a
robbery ring with the boys.

Mother Powell let the talk roll off her, though she
knew it bothered her few true friends and the children
she had tried to help. Inside she was hurt by it though,
and finally the whispering and innuendoes and pointed fingers began to take their toll on her. So when a
she heard of the gold strikes in California a few years
later, she joined the exodus of Forty-Niners.

Many of the folks in Flat Neck, Texas, thought it
scandalous that a single woman, even a widow, would
consider such a thing.

But she did not go to the wild gold mining camps
alone. She was accompanied by her daughter, Amanda, five of the stray children who were still living
under her roof, and an escort of eight heavily armed

men. Three of the men were once errant youths she had taken in. The five other men Mother Powell had helped in various ways. They were glad to escort her, despite knowing that they, too, would be talked about in Flat Neck.

Despite her status as a widow, and despite her natural beauty, she was never molested, even when she set up a restaurant in one rough mining camp after another. She seemed to have a knack of inspiring confidence in most people. For some reason, that kept the men at bay. No one could ever figure it out, but after a while, people began to accept it as a fact.

She started in Sacramento, but eventually moved on to some of the mining camps. She always made out well, what with the amount of gold being pulled from the Sierra Nevada. But she spent almost as much as she made, caring for the motherless children who roamed the rugged mountains.

Mother Powell also began to get a small reputation among the miners for being a soft touch when they were down and out. The miners considered her their own, and guarded their "secret" well.

Still, she tired of the harsh weather and harsher life of the Sierra Nevada and longed to move back east. She liked mountains in general, but these huge, brooding peaks left her melancholy more often than not. She wanted mountains like she was used to from her girlhood. One day she just packed it up. With two of her young men escorting her and her daughter, she began the long trek east.

But somehow she had gotten waylaid by the beauty of the Sangre de Cristo Mountains. She sampled the fare in Cimarron and decided she could provide better victuals. She opened another restaurant and boarding house. But this time, she vowed she would not help out any waifs.

She could not hold to her promise, though the out-of-the-way nature of Cimarron meant there were fewer children to help. And with her reputation for charity left back in the Sierra Nevada, she settled in to live the rest of her life in peace and quiet.

Calhoun was one of the people Mother Powell had helped over the years. He had never talked of it to anyone, but she had nursed him back to health once after he had been shot and seriously wounded. When he had recovered, Mother Powell had given him a stake, enough to get back to Kansas Territory and take up his trade of hunting and scouting again.

Calhoun was not a man to let the burden of obligation bother him overly much. But he felt he owed Mother Agatha Powell his life. And he was guilty that he never had been able to repay her. He vowed as he trudged up the dusty street in Cimarron that he would pay her back, come hell or high water. He needed a stake, and knew he would get it simply for the asking.

The asking would be hard, but he could do it. Then he would do anything in his power to pay her back and then some.

CHAPTER

* 7 *

Calhoun pushed wearily through the door of the restaurant and stopped, giving his eyes time to adjust to the gloominess of the interior.

The place was almost empty. There were twelve tables, but only two were occupied, one by two burly teamsters and another by a down-and-out old man. All three men glanced at Calhoun momentarily, their eyes reflecting either indifference or a moment of fear. Then they went back to their eating.

An attractive young woman was clearing plates from another table. She, too, had looked around at the sound of the door opening. She took in Calhoun with a swift, sure glance. Distaste flickered across her pretty face for a moment. She had no liking for gunmen or saddle tramps. This one looked like both, she thought. And worse, he looked about at the end of his rope. Such men were often dangerous, she knew from experience. She forced a wan smile onto her full, pouting lips and said in a pleasant voice, "Take a seat, mister, I'll be with you directly."

Calhoun watched in appreciation as the young woman finished grabbing the dishes and began hauling them away. Calhoun thought there was something tantalizingly familiar about her, but he could not pin it down. So he pushed the nagging thought away and just stood for another few seconds, enjoying the view of the woman.

She was fairly tall, with full, round hips and a swelling bosom. Chestnut brown hair cascaded in a waterfall over shoulders that were a little too broad for a woman's. Her face, Calhoun had seen in the brief look he had gotten, was pale, with well-defined cheekbones, pouty lips and a strong, straight nose. He assumed that she was one of Mother Powell's girls helping out in the restaurant for whatever reason.

Calhoun shuffled toward a table. He dropped the heavy saddle next to a chair with a thud and plopped into the chair. He rolled a cigarette. As he returned the pouch of tobacco to his shirt pocket, he noted that he had barely enough left for one more. He scraped a match on the table and fired up the paper tube of tobacco.

The young woman came and stood by the table. She barely hid her disgust at Calhoun's shabby appearance. But she asked evenly, "What'll it be?"

"What do you got?"

"Buffalo steak, elk, venison."

"Fresh?"

"All of it," the woman said. She was insulted that someone would question the quality of her food.

"Elk steak, then. The biggest you got. Yams. Biscuits, too. Coffee."

"That it?" the woman asked.

Calhoun looked up at her. Something terribly sad marred the beauty of her face. "Just one more thing. . ."

"I know," the woman said with a sigh, "you ain't got

no money and you're lookin' for a free meal." She nodded firmly. "Reckon I can still do such things for those who need it. And you sure look like you need it."

Calhoun's eyes narrowed. "Unless your prices've gone up considerably," he said, trying to keep the pained anger out of his voice, "I can pay for it."

"Oh," the woman said, somewhat abashed. "Then what. . . ?"

"I was wonderin' where Mother Powell was. Did she sell this place and y'all just kept the name?"

The woman suddenly started crying. Tears spilled down her smooth cheeks and dripped off her chin down onto her bodice. Calhoun was taken aback—an unusual thing for him—and a tinge of concern wedged itself into his guts. He waited patiently while silent sobs racked the woman.

Finally the sobs quivered to a halt and the tears slowed to a trickle. "She's. . . She was. . ."

The woman stopped and sucked in a jagged breath. "She's dead," she finally managed to say flatly.

"Damn," Calhoun breathed. A sense of loss flickered in his stomach. "Sorry, ma'am," he apologized.

The woman nodded. "It's all right," she mumbled. She pulled a cloth from the pocket of her apron and dabbed at her eyes then blew her nose. But she kept the wadded up ball of cloth in her tight fist.

"How?" Calhoun asked quietly. He figured Mother Powell to have been only in her forties. Not all that old. He felt an iciness as worry settled in.

"Killed." The woman's voice was barely discernible.

"Who? How?" Calhoun demanded quietly. Flames of rage had replaced the worry. Now that he knew, there was no more time for worry. But rage, that was another thing. He wondered how anyone could have killed such a fine woman.

"You want to eat, don't you? I got to get the order back to the cook." She began to turn away.

Calhoun's hand snaked out and grabbed the woman's wrist. "I ain't ate a real meal in more'n a week, girl," he snarled. "I can go a bit longer without one. I'm more interested in what happened to Mother Powell."

The woman looked down at him. Her eyes were filled with liquid, but her quivering lids held the tears in.

"Men like me don't have friends," Calhoun said quietly, without regret. "But I considered Mother Powell as close to one as I'll ever have. She helped me out some years ago." He wanted to say more, but he didn't know what so he clamped his mouth closed.

After only a moment's hesitation, the woman nodded. She had seen something in this well-armed hardcase that she felt she could trust. She felt certain she had judged him too harshly at first because of his tattered, dirty clothes and the flat, deadly look in his eyes.

"No reason you should wait longer. I'll give your order to the cook and then come back and tell you."

Calhoun nodded. As the woman turned away, he called out, "Ma'am." She looked over her shoulder at him. "What's your name?"

"Amanda Powell." She paused. "Mother Powell was my ma." She hurried off.

She was back in a few minutes. She nervously

pulled up a chair at Calhoun's table. She sat and folded her small, dainty hands on the table.

Calhoun waited a bit, then said softly, "Tell me, Miss Amanda. What happened to Mother Powell?"

Amanda looked at him, her eyes swimming in painful tears. She breathed raggedly a few times, then said, "It was just over a week ago." She shook her head, not wanting to relive the pain and horror of that day.

Calhoun waited her out. Pressing her now would do no good, he knew. He sat quietly. He rolled his last cigarette and tossed the empty pouch to the other side of the table. He had wanted to save the last one for after his supper but he figured he would need it now.

"Ma was workin' here in the restaurant like she always did. The place was crowded and we were all busy. I was in the kitchen when suddenly these seven tough-lookin' *hombres* walked in." She closed her eyes tightly, trying to blot out the picture her own words had conjured up but was unsuccessful.

The lids lifted, bringing out the bright blue, red-rimmed eyes. Her hurt was reflected deep in those blue pools. But her voice was even and held little inflection.

"They chased out most of the other customers, threatenin' to shoot them all down. Then they . . . they just sat and started eatin' other folks' food.

"Ma tried talkin' to them, tryin' to tell them they could have whatever they wanted but they ought to show some manners. It seemed she was gettin' through to them. Then . . . "

A scrawny, poorly clothed, buck-toothed black woman suddenly stuck a plate of food in front of Calhoun's face. He cast a dark, angry glance at her.

The woman's eyes widened with fright, and she backed hurriedly away.

"Be more mindful of folks, Melba," Amanda scolded, though not too harshly.

"Yes'm," the black woman mumbled. She turned and ran on bare feet back to the kitchen.

Calhoun began cutting up his steak. Amanda watched him for a moment, then asked, "Want me to go on?"

"Soon."

Amanda waited, wondering why. Then Melba returned, balancing a platter of biscuits, a bowl of butter, and a mug on one arm. She carried a pot of coffee in the other hand. She set the items down carefully, face worried.

"Thank you, Melba," Calhoun said politely.

The black woman still looked scared. She bobbed her head in acknowledgement and then scurried back toward the kitchen.

Calhoun stuck a forkful of elk steak into his mouth. As he chewed, he said, "Go on."

"Well," Amanda said slowly, "they started throwin' food and such. Ma gave them what-for, and the one who seemed to be the leader commenced gettin' nasty."

Amanda bit her lower lip nervously. "I started to come on out, aimin' to help Ma. But she turned and I could tell in her eyes she wanted me to stay behind."

She was crying again. She looked helpless, and she

knew it. That infuriated her. She had gotten the best from both Ezra and Agatha Powell. She was usually strong and determined, able to stay calm in any crisis. But this was something she had never counted on.

Calhoun ate silently, letting Amanda get it out of her system. He knew it was the best thing for her right now.

Amanda bit back the bile that rose in her throat. "They started slappin' Ma around some, hootin' and laughin'. Then they all. . . they all. . . Good Lord, those animals."

She choked on the hard words and the anger. "How could men do. . . such. . ." She broke off again, her breath rattling in and out.

"You don't have to say it," Calhoun offered. He knew full well what Amanda was trying to say. It made knots of sickness in his stomach knowing there were men in this world who were capable of rape. He could not understand how they could do such a thing to a kindly woman like Mother Powell. He only knew that such men existed. And that he would have to try to make sure this particular group of them did not exist much longer.

Amanda nodded, unable to speak for a while. Then she went on in a voice that was raspy. "After they . . . they . . . were done . . ." She moaned, unaware that she did so. "They just pulled their pistols and . . . and. . . ."

She ground to a stop. Her racking sobs reminded her of the fusillade of gunfire that erupted. She could see her mother dance as the bullets plundered her body. But Mother Powell had died never making a sound; never cursing her attackers; never screaming out in hate at them.

Amanda Powell had done all those things for Mother Powell. As the seven men had stomped toward the door, aware that the gunfire would be bringing people soon, Amanda rushed out of the kitchen.

She had knelt in the pool of blood on the restaurant floor and cradled her mother's blood-soaked body to her breast. And she had screamed and cursed—words she didn't even know she knew—and called upon God to smite these evil bastards down.

Later, when her mother was buried, Amanda prayed that God would send someone to do His bidding, to seek retribution in His name for this senseless crime.

Amanda remembered those prayers now. Suddenly her tears and sobs stopped. She looked at Calhoun with sudden understanding.

C H A P T E R

* 8 *

Calhoun pushed the plate away from him. The food had been good and filling, but it still sat in his stomach like a rock. He felt cold inside at the heinousness of what had been done to Mother Agatha Powell.

He leaned back in his chair, wishing he had a little more tobacco left. He glanced at the empty tobacco pouch but resisted the urge to check it just in case.

Amanda Powell saw the look. Despite her fears and heartache, she was conscious of what it signified. She glanced over and spotted Melba watching from around the corner of the kitchen door. Amanda crooked her finger.

Melba edged out, fear knotting up her stomach. "Yes'm?" she mumbled as she inched up to the table.

"Fetch Mister . . . " She turned to Calhoun. "Just what is your name, anyway?" She was flustered, realizing that she had been pouring her heart out to this man without even knowing his name.

"Wade Calhoun."

Amanda nodded. "Fetch Mister Calhoun some tobacco and papers." Once more she looked directly in his eyes. "Unless you'd rather have a cigar?"

"Nope."

"Fetch the tobacco then, Melba. And be quick about it, girl."

Melba ran off. Calhoun and Amanda sat in silence. The two teamsters had gone some time ago, and the old man, realizing that he would be getting nothing more for free today, had gone, too. The saddle tramp and Amanda had the place to themselves.

Melba returned quickly and placed a pouch of tobacco, a package of rolling papers, and a box of matches on the table at Calhoun's elbow. The latter had been her idea, and she was quite proud of having thought of it.

Calhoun absently nodded his thanks and began building a smoke. He blew out a cloud, enjoying the bite of the harsh tobacco on the back of his throat. "You know who it was?" he asked suddenly, surprising Amanda.

"Not all of them. A man named Garth Nichols is the leader, I found out. I also know that Warren Shoemaker, Harry Graham, Jaron Cridlow, and Conley Muir were with them. We don't know the other two."

"Know anything about 'em?"

"Not much. I heard Nichols had been in prison several times. Graham, too." She shrugged her shoulders. The motion created other bodily movements that distracted Calhoun momentarily.

"Tell me what they look like," Calhoun urged softly.

Amanda shook her head and looked at the table. Her long hair swung forward, covering most of her face. She was abashed. The faces of those seven men were burned into her brain, but she could not put those faces into words for others to see.

"It's all right," Calhoun said gruffly. "A posse go after them that day?"

"Yep." Amanda's head came up. "Sheriff McCloskey headed out with more than two dozen men less than two hours after it . . . " She paused, catching her breath.

Calhoun stubbed out his cigarette and finished the last of his coffee.

"Where are my manners?" Amanda asked, angry at herself. She stood and walked toward a cabinet near the back of the restaurant. She opened it and pulled out a bottle of whiskey and a glass. She brought them back to the table, filled the glass from the bottle and sat.

Calhoun picked up the glass of amber liquid. He held it out toward Amanda a little way, in a sort of salute. Then he swallowed it down. He refilled the glass. "The posse?" Calhoun hinted.

Amanda nodded. "Three men got killed—includin' two of Sheriff McCloskey's deputies. The rest turned tail and headed back here."

"They tried goin' back out after 'em?"

Amanda shook her head. "Most of the men're too afraid. The others figure they'd never find Garth Nichols and the others anyway."

Calhoun nodded. He was angry at it, but at the same time, he understood the reasoning. Most of these men had families or jobs, or both. They could not afford to go traipsing off for God only knew how long chasing the fading wisps of outlaws. No matter how much they might want to catch the miscreants.

Calhoun, on the other hand, had no such problems.

He had determined as soon as Amanda had told him that Mother Powell had been killed that he would go after the killers. He could do no less. It was not much, but it was the only way he could think of to pay Mother Powell back for the help she had given him.

And he could—and would—take as long as necessary. After hearing of how Agatha had been killed, he was more determined than ever to see those men dead. He would follow them to the back end of hell, if need be, to visit righteous revenge upon them.

"You plannin' to go after them?" Amanda asked, in a voice both frightened and enraged.

"Yes, ma'am."

She looked at the hard, pockmarked face and the flat, deadly eyes. She knew he was telling the truth. She shuddered. It would take a man as hard and heartless as the men who had killed her mother to catch them. Wade Calhoun was, she thought, such a man.

"Thank you," she whispered.

"Ain't done nothin' yet." Calhoun jerked down another shot of whiskey. "You know where these animals might be found?"

Amanda shook her head. "They don't come around Cimarron much. They'd only been seen here once or twice before that . . . day." She shrugged, irritated at the helplessness that came from a lack of knowledge.

Calhoun sat thinking. It seemed impossible on the face of it. The seven men could be anywhere between the Mexican border and Canada, from California to the Mississippi River. Finding them might prove to be impossible.

But there were ways. Someone in town must know

something. Someone must have had dealings with the men before. It was simply a matter of finding that person or persons and convincing them to reveal what they knew. Calhoun considered himself very persuasive when the need arose.

"Don't you fret none, ma'am," Calhoun finally said quietly. "They'll pay for this."

His eyes took on a far-off look and Amanda felt a twinge of fear. This man was not one to get too close to. He had the scent of death on him.

"When will you start?"

"Soon's I get some things. A horse, supplies and such."

"You have the cash?" Amanda asked. She had the momentary thought that Calhoun had been acting aggrieved by Mother Powell's death, and that it was all to get some money from her. But she knew in her heart that it was not so. Still, it might be wise to take some precautions.

"Not enough." Calhoun wanted to vomit. He would rather shoot himself in the foot than have to admit that to anyone, least of all an attractive young woman. But this was not the time nor the place for pride. If he was to find Mother Powell's killers, he would need Amanda's help.

"How much you got?"

Calhoun stood, fighting back the shame. He reached into his pocket and pulled out all the money he had. He dropped it on the table. He turned his pockets inside out to show Amanda that he was hiding nothing. He sat back down.

Amanda counted the money. "Ain't much, is it?" she

said, figuring that he must be abashed at all this.

"Nope," Calhoun said sourly. He paused. "You can look through the saddlebags, if you're of a mind to."

"No, sir," Amanda said seriously. "You didn't need to empty your pockets neither. You could've just told me."

Calhoun shrugged.

Amanda shoved the money toward Calhoun. "Keep it. You might need it on the trail," she said firmly. "I'll make sure you're outfitted proper."

"Might cost a pretty penny."

"It'll be worth every cent."

Calhoun nodded.

"What's first?"

Calhoun lifted a foot and showed Amanda the bottom of his boots.

Amanda nodded. "First the general store. You could use some new clothes from top to bottom. You need powder and ball and such?"

"Never hurts to have some," Calhoun said dryly.

"Let's go."

Calhoun polished off the glass of whiskey and stood. He bent and reached for his saddle.

"Leave it," Amanda ordered politely. "Melba!" she called. When the young black woman came out of the kitchen and stood scuffling her feet on the floor, Amanda said, "Take Mister Calhoun's gear to the big back room of the boarding house. Mind you treat it well."

"Yes'm."

"Shall we go, Mister Calhoun?"

"Yes'm," Calhoun said dryly.

They marched outside and up the alley to the main street and turned right. Several doors up was a large, well-outfitted mercantile store. Amanda led the way in. Like her mother, Amanda Powell was strong-willed and at least partly unfettered by convention.

Amanda introduced Adolph Blenheim, who owned the store. Then she stepped back while Calhoun ordered whatever he felt he needed. The list was not long: three pairs of pants and three shirts; three bandannas; new hide boots; and a hat. Some socks and longhandles completed his outfit.

Calhoun bought several tins of DuPont's powder and several bars of Galena lead, plus nitrate paper and percussion caps. He also arranged to pick up some foodstuffs—a little salted beef, jerky, flour, beans, bacon, and coffee—when he was ready to ride out.

Calhoun put on the new boots, tossing the old ones away from him with disgust. He stood. "Better," he grunted and looked at Amanda. "A horse?"

She nodded. "Have these things delivered to the boardinghouse, Mister Blenheim," she said.

Calhoun almost grinned. She not only had her mother's looks, which is what had made her seem familiar to him at first, she also had her mother's will. She could give orders and know they would be obeyed. Amanda Powell was an impressive young woman.

Outside, they crossed the street and took a side street, following it to the end. A fragile-looking barn and a large corral of wood poles spread out there. Just to the side of the barn was an open-air blacksmith's shop.

"Mornin', Miss Powell," a short, broad man said. He

wiped his forehead on a brawny forearm at the end of which dangled a short, blunt hammer.

"Mornin', Horatio. We need a horse."

"Take your pick." He pointed to the corral with the hammer.

Amanda nodded. She turned, but Calhoun was already climbing into the corral. He moved slowly from animal to animal. He checked each horse's legs and chest and teeth. He moved his hands along each animal's hide, feeling for old wounds or breaks or mal-treatment.

Finally he chose a blotchy bay with a white nose and white stockings. It was an unprepossessing look-ing horse, but Calhoun chose the animal for its stami-na, not its looks.

"How much?" he asked.

"Seventy-five," the liveryman said without blinking.

Amanda reached for her money pouch, but Cal-houn's hand on her arm stopped her. "That's rob-bery," Calhoun said simply.

Horatio Smith glared angrily at Calhoun. But then he dropped his eyes. He had seen something in Cal-houn that left him distinctly uncomfortable. "Sixty."

"Nag ain't worth more than twenty."

They settled on forty, with a sack of oats thrown in. Amanda handed over the cash, and then she and Cal-houn headed back toward the restaurant. As they walked, Amanda asked, "When will you be leavin'?"

"Soon's I can find out which way to go." He rubbed a hand across the stubble on his chin. "Reckon I ought to see if the sheriff can tell me anything useful." He sounded doubtful.

CHAPTER

✳ 9 ✳

Calhoun looked without seeming to as two drunken men staggered out of a saloon up the street a little way. He instinctively sensed that they might cause trouble, but he did not let on to Amanda, who was walking next to him. Amanda seemed distracted and was not paying much attention to her surroundings.

Calhoun took Amanda's elbow lightly in hand and pushed ever so gently. "Let's cross here, ma'am," he said quietly.

"But my place is down there," she said, jerking her small, pointy chin down the street in the direction they had been heading. She thought that perhaps because Calhoun was new in Cimarron, he might have lost his bearings.

Calhoun said nothing. He just kept up the slight pressure, steering Amanda across the street. She glanced up at him sharply, ready to argue with him about it. But she kept her mouth shut when she saw the harder-than-usual look on Calhoun's face. She followed his eyes and saw the two drunks.

The two men were standing in front of the saloon, weaving. Raucous whoops erupted from their mouths and they were unlimbering their pistols.

Amanda was concerned but not frightened. Here and elsewhere she had seen too many instances of men getting liquored up and firing off a few rounds in celebration of whatever it was buzzing around in their whiskey-besotted brains. They would whoop it up a bit and then Sheriff McCloskey would show up and escort them off to the calaboose where they could sleep it off. They would pay for their exuberance with a hangover and a small fine, like as not.

Of course, it was not unknown for an innocent person walking down the street to be hit—and sometimes killed—by their random gunfire. But she figured the chances of that were slim.

She and Calhoun were on the other side of the street now, still walking steadily but without haste. Calhoun kept his eyes fixed on the men. He, too, had seen such activity. And while he was not worried about it, he was not about to let himself be killed by a stray bullet. As he walked, he kept his right thumb hooked lightly on his gunbelt, leaving his hand inches from one of the Colt Dragoons.

The two men fired their pistols up in the air a couple of times. Each shot was accompanied by a whoop, a holler and peals of drunken laughter.

Suddenly a man with a shiny badge on his chest appeared. He was a fairly large man, almost as tall as Calhoun, with a big chest, broad belly, and hard-looking, florid face. He seemed to have no neck, just a big, round head atop massive shoulders. He had a large-bore six-shooter in one meaty fist.

"That McCloskey?" Calhoun asked.

"Yes," Amanda answered. She was relieved. The

gunfire had made her a little nervous. Now that McCloskey was around, she felt more secure.

Calhoun slowed his pace, interested in watching McCloskey in action. Calhoun figured he would have to deal with McCloskey sooner or later if he was to learn anything about the men who had killed Mother Powell. He wanted to see just how good this sheriff was.

His first impression of the sheriff was favorable.

McCloskey marched fearlessly up to the two drunks from their blind side. Without hesitation, he cracked one of them on the crown of the head with his pistol barrel. The man went down, dropping his revolver. In an odd lull in the normal noise of the town, Calhoun thought he heard the man moan from all the way across the street.

McCloskey jammed the muzzle of his pistol into the other man's ribs at the back. He said something that Calhoun could not hear, and the drunk uncocked his gun and handed it over to the lawman. McCloskey shoved the man's pistol in his belt, then slid his own revolver into the holster.

Calhoun stopped to watch, interested. He was aware that several men had come to the door of the saloon in front of which he was standing. They, too, were watching.

Amanda walked two steps farther before realizing Calhoun was not with her anymore. She halted and moved back to his side. "What's wrong?" she asked, worried.

Calhoun shook his head. "Nothin'." He was still rather interested in the lawman's actions and abilities and just wanted to see the short episode out to its conclusion.

McCloskey reached down and grabbed the downed man by the scruff of his shirt. He started to haul the drunk up. At the same time, the other drunk lurched around and slammed McCloskey on the side of the head with his two hands clasped into one fist.

McCloskey went down, landing atop the first drunk, slightly stunned. As the lawman fell, the drunk who had hit him snatched the sheriff's pistol from his holster.

The downed man shoved the sheriff up off him and grabbed his partner's pistol out of McCloskey's gunbelt. He tottered to his feet. His pistol was cocked. The two drunken men aimed their revolvers down at the helpless and unarmed sheriff.

Across the street, Calhoun had reacted instantaneously and without thought as soon as he had seen the one drunken man hit McCloskey. Instinctively, he shoved Amanda hard with his left hand, pushing her toward the door of the saloon behind him. He wanted her out of harm's way should gunfire break out. She stumbled and fell through the swinging half-doors, bouncing off two of the men who had gathered there to watch.

Even as a cry of surprise burst from Amanda's mouth, Calhoun had yanked out one of his Colt Dragoons and was running. There were far too many people in the street for him to risk a shot from where he had been.

Calhoun skidded to a halt halfway across the dusty street. The area between him and the others had cleared as people saw trouble and ran. Calhoun now had a clear line of fire.

He never even considered shouting a warning at the two men. There would not be time, and he wanted the element of surprise. Besides, somewhere in the back of his mind, Calhoun knew that the two men had been given every opportunity to give themselves up peaceably.

Calhoun fired, emptying his Dragoon.

The saddle tramp's first ball broke the gun arm of the man who had slugged McCloskey. The drunk screeched in shock and surprise. His pistol plopped in the dirt.

Calhoun's second and third bullets hit the other drunk square in the chest. A quarter could have covered the two bloody holes just over the heart. Their impact slammed the man back against the wall of the hotel, right next to the large window. The man's arm flew out and shattered the window. He fell sideways amid a shower of broken glass.

The other drunk stood flatfooted, staring down at the sheriff's pistol. He started to kneel to retrieve the weapon with his left hand. Suddenly his head exploded in a spray of brains, blood, and bone. He stood, weaving. Half the back of his head was gone from the power of two .44-caliber balls. The light had gone out of his eyes too. But it took a moment or two for his body to realize it was dead. The thing crumpled in a sloppy heap.

Calhoun jerked out his other Dragoon in his left hand and approached warily. His caution, he found when he checked the two drunks, was unnecessary.

He turned, shoving the Dragoon away. He offered a hand to McCloskey. The whole thing had taken place in the time span of perhaps a dozen heartbeats.

McCloskey was dazed. He was used to sudden gunplay and was even prepared for a quick, violent demise. What had stunned him, though, was his miraculous delivery from certain death. He stared at this man with the hard, solemn face for a few moments. Then he shrugged mentally. This shabbily dressed, deadly looking stranger had saved his life; he could not believe Calhoun would do him any harm. He took Calhoun's hand and let himself be pulled to his feet.

By the time he was standing, McCloskey had recovered his reason. "Obliged," he said quietly.

Calhoun nodded.

"Mind tellin' me who I'm obliged to?"

"Name's Wade Calhoun."

The lawman nodded. "Sheriff John McCloskey," he said in a deep, gruff voice. He held out his hand.

Calhoun took it and pumped the beefy appendage twice. "Know these two?" he asked.

"Nope." He looked at the one nearest him. Bottle flies were already buzzing around the large, jagged hole that had only moments ago been covered by a mat of fine, brown hair. "Couple of drifters, I reckon."

The lawman looked at Calhoun. He had plenty of questions. But he supposed he would never find out who Calhoun really was, or why Calhoun was here, or why Calhoun had saved his life. He shrugged. The questions were not all that important, he decided. "Anything I can do for you, Mister Calhoun?" he asked. "Sort of pay you back a little for your help."

Clint Hawkins

"Answer some questions."

McCloskey looked at Calhoun in surprise. He was used to asking questions, not answering them. "About what?" he asked suspiciously.

"Later," Calhoun said as Amanda walked up.

McCloskey nodded, understanding. Such business should not be conducted either in the presence of a woman or on the public streets of Cimarron.

The young woman looked composed. Even the sight of the man with half his head gone did not seem to faze her. "You all right, Mister Calhoun?" she asked.

"Yes'm."

She stared at him a few seconds. She felt an attraction for this tough, broad-shouldered man. She knew she shouldn't, but that did not lessen the feeling any. She finally tore her eyes away from the pitted face. "And you, Sheriff?"

"Just fine, ma'am," the lawman said easily. "Thanks to your friend here."

McCloskey was still slightly shaken by the incident. No matter how much he had mentally prepared for a sudden, bloody death, the reality of coming so close to it was more than a little disquieting.

CHAPTER

* 10 *

Calhoun settled himself into a chair in Sheriff McCloskey's small, untidy office. The oak chair creaked but otherwise gave the feeling of solidness and support.

Once Calhoun was seated, he rolled a cigarette. He lit it with a match scraped across the sheriff's rough desk. McCloskey set down a cup of harsh, black coffee on the desk in front of his guest and one for himself. He sat. Then he filled and fired up a small, old clay pipe.

"What can I answer for you, Mister Calhoun?" McCloskey asked. He still was uncomfortable about all this. But he was determined not to let any of his uncertainty show.

"Tell me about Mother Powell," Calhoun said in clipped tones. His voice floated to McCloskey through a cloud of cigarette smoke and steam from the coffee.

"What about her?" McCloskey asked tentatively. He wondered how much Calhoun knew. After all, Calhoun had been with Mother Powell's daughter not long ago.

Calhoun glared at the lawman, eyes burning through the fog. "Tell me, dammit," he snarled in a low, menacing voice.

McCloskey gulped. He would admit fear of few men.

He decided here and now that this saddle tramp was one man to fear. He saw what Calhoun had done to the two drunks just a couple of hours ago. And the deadliness in his voice rang in McCloskey's ears.

"What do you know about it?" McCloskey asked. His worry began to spread.

"Miss Amanda told me what happened at the restaurant." Calhoun paused, looking at the glowing tip of his cigarette for a moment. "I want you to tell me what happened afterward."

"Mind if I ask why?"

"Yep."

The coldness in that one little word sent a shudder rippling through the tough sheriff. But it also answered the question for him.

Now, though, he wasn't sure whether that was good or bad. If this hard-edged saddle tramp planned to go gunning for the animals who had savaged Mother Powell, then McCloskey was all for it.

On the other hand, if Calhoun could pull the job off, it would make McCloskey look pretty incompetent. He decided after a few moments that being looked upon as incompetent was a hell of a lot better than being dead. Which is what he figured he would be if he went out after those desperate outlaws alone. Helping Calhoun, he realized, could only benefit everyone.

Still, he was worried. He wasn't sure just how much help he could give Calhoun. And if Calhoun got angry. . .

McCloskey suppressed another shudder. "I don't know all that much," he said, a note of true sadness in his voice. He had liked Mother Powell, and he wanted to be able to do something to avenge her brutalization and death.

"Then tell me what you do know." Calhoun was usually on a short fuse and McCloskey was trying his meager patience already.

"Well, hell," McCloskey said. He rubbed a hand over his face, suddenly weary. "I got a posse up as soon as I could—took less than an hour, I'd say—and set out after those nasty sons a bitches. We caught 'em seven, eight miles out."

He grimaced and his teeth clamped on the pipe, which almost broke. "Damn, I wish I hadn't caught 'em. I lost two deputies and Mister Sprager, the barber." He shook his head in sadness. "They were all good men."

Calhoun sat in stony silence. He cared not a whit for McCloskey's deputies, nor for Mister Sprager. He had not met any of them, and he would waste no sympathy on them. The deputies had been paid lawmen; Mister Sprager had voluntarily joined a posse. They all should have known what the dangers were.

McCloskey grew a little angry at Calhoun's lack of response. But he realized that letting emotion get the better of him now would be foolish—and dangerous.

"Anyway," he said with a sigh, "those bastards riddled us with gunfire and then took off again. The fight went out of my boys about then. We brought our dead and wounded back to town." He shrugged, signifying that that was it. He was not proud of it, but he figured he had done the only reasonable thing under the circumstances.

"You didn't get up more men and go back after 'em?" Calhoun asked derisively.

"Nope." McCloskey looked ashamed. He would

have ridden on right then, given his choice. But he would have done so alone, since none of the other men in the posse would go with him. When they had returned to town, he tried to get up another posse and failed. He even had tried to get a federal deputy marshal to come help, but had been put off. He was told that the deputy United States marshal would be there in a month. Or two.

The lawman thought of explaining all that to the saddle tramp. But then he decided that Calhoun would not care about any of it. So McCloskey saved his breath.

The little information McCloskey had provided backed up what Amanda had told Calhoun. But that didn't make him like it any. "You should've gone alone," he said in accusatory tones.

"They don't pay me enough for such things," McCloskey said uncomfortably.

Calhoun glared. McCloskey returned the look.

"Forty bucks a month ain't enough for committin' suicide," the sheriff said defensively. He hoped he kept any note of doubt out of his voice.

Calhoun understood, but he did not like it. He would not show the lawman any mercy. "It ain't the amount of money," he said viciously.

"I know," McCloskey said quietly. He looked pained. "But I've got the welfare of everyone in Cimarron to look out for. Even if I wanted to go out there after those bastards alone—and I did want to—I would've been derelict in my duty. Hell, that would've left Cimarron with no protection."

McCloskey paused, chewing on the scraggly ends of

his graying mustache. "No matter how much I cared for Mother Powell, I had to think about the other folks in town," he added.

"Well, I sure as hell don't," Calhoun said with a low, growling note.

McCloskey grinned viciously. It was what the lawman wanted to hear from Calhoun.

"So tell me where I can find the sons of bitches who did it," Calhoun added.

"Got no idea," McCloskey admitted, crestfallen. He had been filled with elation at the knowledge that Calhoun would head out after Garth Nichols and the others. But that came crashing to a halt. The Nichols bunch were like ghosts; wisps of smoke in the night. They appeared out of nowhere every once in a while, created some hellacious mischief and then faded into the mountains again.

Calhoun stared hard at the lawman. "You've got to know something."

McCloskey shrugged, bitterly disappointed in himself. "They just come and go," he said lamely. "Nobody's ever been able to follow 'em to find out where they hole up."

"You ever had a good tracker out after 'em?"

"Once. Some guy named Parker. He was supposed to be one of the best."

"He is good," Calhoun admitted. He did not voice his opinion that while he thought Aram Parker was good, he wasn't as good as the saddle tramp himself.

McCloskey shrugged his meaty shoulders. "He might be, but he didn't have no luck neither."

Calhoun grunted in annoyance. He was determined

to find and kill these men. He was bound by the vow he had made to himself. Now he was to be thwarted by the sheriff's inefficiency. His mood soured even further.

McCloskey saw the look on Calhoun's face, and his fear heightened. He figured Calhoun to be one hell of a deadly man in such a mood. McCloskey's mind raced, as he tried to think of something that would help; something that would deflect the blazing anger in those dark, brooding eyes that stabbed deep into his innards.

"Wait a minute," he said, brightening minutely. "There's been some suspicion that Willy Becker—he runs the billiards parlor down the street—is related to Garth Nichols in some way."

"How?" Calhoun's voice was as cold as a January blizzard and just as deadly.

"Nobody knows for sure."

Calhoun grunted in annoyance.

"But folks say he's Nichols's half-brother. They had the same ma, the rumor goes."

"You think he'd know where Nichols and the other bastards usually hole up?"

McCloskey shrugged again. "If—and it's a mighty big if—the rumor's true, Becker might know something."

He rubbed a beefy paw across his face. Times like this, he wished he was living somewhere else, doing something, anything else, for a living. But he was stuck with the job and would do it as best he knew how. "If he don't, I don't know where in hell we'll find out anything."

"Ain't you questioned him?"

"Not directly." McCloskey squirmed under Calhoun's hard gaze. "I've tried doin' so indirectly, just hintin' around. But that's all I can do." He shrugged in his helplessness. "All we got to go on is a rumor. I've got to have more than that to question a man about something so serious."

"Bullshit," Calhoun snapped. He was frustrated, and that always boosted the anger that constantly simmered just below the surface.

"We got laws here, Mister Calhoun," McCloskey said plaintively. "We've got to abide by 'em."

"I don't have to abide by no goddamn stupid laws," Calhoun snarled, anger bubbling over. He shoved up from the chair, sending it crashing backward to the floor. He glared at McCloskey. "And I'm warnin' you, boy, don't come tryin' to enforce them laws on me."

Calhoun spit on the floor, spun and stalked out, his back stiff with rage.

CHAPTER

✴ 11 ✴

Wade Calhoun strolled nonchalantly into Becker's Billiards Parlor, thankful to be out of the cloudy, rain-filled night. Lightning provided occasional illumination, but did nothing to dispel the chill. Thunder rumbled in small, cacophonous waves over the town of Cimarron.

The billiards parlor was far less ostentatious than its name implied. It was dimly lit with smoky, foul-smelling lanterns against the dark of the cloudy night. Cigarette smoke added to the dense fog in the place.

Eight tables, imported from St. Louis, a sign on one wall proudly proclaimed, filled most of the room. A small bar, with a tiny but impressively built back bar, snuggled up against the left-hand wall as Calhoun entered.

Calhoun took a quick, thorough glance around and headed for the bar. He ordered a bottle of rye and laid two silver dollars on the surface of the bar. The bottle and a glass materialized. The bartender swept up the coins and disappeared. Calhoun poured a drink and sipped it.

All Calhoun knew about Becker was a short description Amanda Powell had given him earlier. So he stood calmly at the bar, sipping his rye, smoking cigarettes, and listening. He wanted to be able to take notice if someone addressed Becker, though he saw no one matching the description he had.

After a little while Calhoun picked up his bottle and glass and wandered around the room. He stopped at a table, watched for a few minutes and then moved on to the next table. He had little interest in the games that were in progress, but he thought it wouldn't hurt to try to glean some fragment of information that might be revealed accidentally.

He learned nothing of any importance to him.

An hour later, a dapper, well-dressed man entered and walked straight behind the bar.

Calhoun snapped alert and moseyed toward the bar. Just as he got there and set his bottle and glass down, he heard the bartender say, ". . . pretty good tonight, Mister Becker."

Calhoun nodded imperceptibly, acknowledging the information to himself. Becker was a short, portly, well-dressed man who seemed cocky. The cloying fragrance of too much lime water wafted heavily from his pinkish cheeks.

Calhoun watched for only a few moments before he drained his shot glass. He jammed the cork into the bottle and walked out, swinging the bottle loosely in his hand.

His room had been cleaned up. Earlier he had taken a bath, his first in months, and then dressed in his new duds. Amanda Powell had seen to it that all was taken care of. Then he had gone to see Sheriff McCloskey. He had been there only a short while before returning to his room. He had taken the opportunity then to nap a little, waiting for the darkness to come. He had learned long ago to snatch a nap whenever and wherever possible.

Calhoun set the bottle down and turned the lamp up a little. He poured a drink and sat in an old, hand-carved chair with his feet up on the small table. He rolled a cigarette and sipped the poor rye whiskey.

As the clock struck midnight, Calhoun corked the bottle and stood. He checked his pistols one last time. Then he turned the lamp down and left the room, quietly closing the door behind him.

Calhoun waited in the shadows at the corner of the billiards parlor. He was at the lip of an alley, just beyond the ring of light thrown by the lantern on the post nearby. It was still drizzling and the thunder and lightning continued their symphony of light and sound.

The bartender came out of the billiards parlor and stopped. He breathed deep of the warm, moist air for a few moments before strolling casually down the street. A few minutes later the other helpers came out of the building and hurried off in different directions. Even the two who passed within a foot of Calhoun did not know he was there.

Calhoun took a quick glance around and then walked swiftly along the front of the building to the double doors at the center. He pushed in and shut the door.

"One of you boys forget something?" a friendly voice asked from behind the bar.

Calhoun moved soundlessly in that direction.

"Someone there?" The voice now held a strong note of worry and fear.

Calhoun was at the bar, and slid silently behind it. Suddenly he was behind the short, plump man. Becker's lime water was masked a little by the smell of growing fear.

"Evenin', Mister Becker," Calhoun said quietly.

The smaller man leaped around, face glimmering strangely white in the dim light cast by the only lantern left burning. He gasped and his hand flew up to his mouth.

"Who the hell are you?" Becker asked, voice quavering. He fought for control.

"Name's Wade Calhoun." The saddle tramp's voice was calm and even.

"What do you want here?" Becker seemed a little bolder.

"Information."

"Get the hell out of here." Becker drew himself up. He had had trouble with drifters and other no-accounts before. He was not afraid of this man. He could not really see Calhoun, though he sensed the saddle tramp was a big, strong fellow.

"After I've got what I come for."

"I'm tellin' you, mister, you best get out of here now. The sheriff'll be along here in a few minutes." Becker felt a little smug now.

"Not tonight he won't," Calhoun said evenly. He had earlier asked Amanda to take a message to McCloskey warning the lawman to keep away from the billiards parlor tonight. He assumed McCloskey had enough sense to heed the warning.

Becker gulped. If what Calhoun had said was true, he could be in deep trouble. "You want money?" he asked, mouth dry. "Go 'head, take it. All I got. Just don't hurt me."

"I don't want your goddamn money," Calhoun snarled. "Just some information."

"What information?" Becker was confused. Most men like Calhoun would be here to rob him. He could not fathom what kind of information this tough-talking man could want from him.

"Tell me where I can find Garth Nichols and his cronies."

"Who?" Becker sighed in relief. He knew the rumors about his being related to the outlaw Garth Nichols. He had been hearing them for a while, and they never had gotten to be more than that. Even the sheriff had tried, badly, to talk about it without saying anything directly. Becker thought that had been funny. It was so easy, he thought, to pull the wool over that plodding lawman's eyes.

He figured it should be as easy to do the same with this saddle tramp. He smiled smugly.

The smile dropped like a pebble down a well as searing pain burned through the side of his head. It had come so fast that he never even had time to scream before the shock took over. Nor had he seen the lightning fast bowie blade.

Becker brought his left hand up and felt the side of his head. It came away coated with fresh blood. The sudden, shocking realization that he no longer had an ear on that side of his head caused him to open his mouth to scream.

Calhoun still held the bloody bowie in his right hand. He was set to smash his left hand into Becker's face to shut him up. But a massive crack of thunder that seemed to roll over the town for an eternity drowned out the animal cry of pain.

"I'm a man of limited patience, Mister Becker," Calhoun said when the thunder died. "You have information I want. I will get it. Believe me."

Becker's eyes seemed as big as supper plates. His breath came with difficulty, in rasping jerks caused by his overwhelming fright.

Calhoun waited a few moments as the dapper little man tried to spit out the fear that clogged his mouth and throat. After a moment, he asked fearfully, "You won't kill me?"

"Don't plan to."

"I don't really know what you want to know," Becker said in a shaking voice. He quickly held up his hand to ward off any more knife action on Calhoun's part. "Really. I don't." His face was constricted with fear and pain.

"I thought takin' an ear would be sufficient to loosen your tongue," Calhoun said almost distractedly.

"But I don't know what you want to know!" Becker wailed.

"Guess I could've been wrong," Calhoun said, as if he had not heard Becker. He had no doubts that Becker knew something. He could read it in the natty man's eyes and manner.

"I don't know nothin'!" Becker's voice rose.

Calhoun shrugged. "No matter. I'll just have to start removin' other body parts. . ."

Becker vomited as the bowie blade suddenly

touched his crotch.

"Talk," Calhoun said harshly.

Becker's mouth flapped as he tried to form words. There was no denying that Calhoun would do as he was threatening to do. Becker desperately wanted to speak before the knife bit into his privates. But the words were not coming. Sweat poured down his face as he prayed for the gift of speech.

The gift was given suddenly, and a screeching jumble of words tumbled forth. "I'll talk! Lord, Christ. I'll talk. I'll tell you! Jesus, just move the knife away. Please!" He was crying and his legs trembled from fear. He thought he might collapse.

Blessedly, the knife was removed. Becker drew in a shaky breath that rattled around his sobs of terror.

"Talk," Calhoun commanded.

"Drink first?" Becker asked hopefully.

"Talk." Calhoun's voice was as hard as iron and as foreboding as the night.

Becker gulped. "Garth's my half-brother," he said weakly. "Just like everyone suspected." He licked his lips. "I don't want nothin' to do with him most times, but . . . well, hell, I'm afraid of that *loco* son of a bitch."

Becker paused again to see how he was doing. But Calhoun's solid bulk had not moved. It was as intimidating as ever.

"He . . . he. . . " Becker stopped again, sputtering. The cloying fog of fear left him befuddled, unable to think. "I could really use a drink, mister," he said, a pleading note in his voice.

With his left hand, Calhoun uncorked a bottle and poured a glass of whiskey. He was not watching the liquid since he was keeping his eyes on Becker, so the liquor overflowed. Calhoun poured a little out onto the bar, took a sip and then flung the remainder in Becker's face.

"Talk, you son of a bitch," he warned. "I won't tell you again."

A little of the whiskey had landed on the spot where Becker had shortly before had an ear. It stung like hellfire, but the owner of the billiards parlor was too scared to put his hand up to wipe it away. Instead, he licked up the few drops he could reach with his tongue.

He took a deep breath. He had thought perhaps he could get out of this by stalling, but now he was sure that would not work. He figured his half-brother would kill him sure as all get-out if he found out that Becker had talked. But Becker knew for sure that Calhoun would kill him here and now, without a thought.

"Best bet is Cimarron Canyon. Garth takes the boys up there most often. They either camp out in the forest up along the Cimarron River, or in some of the caves up on the Palisades there."

"Where's the canyon?"

"About halfway between here and Taos. You can't miss it."

The dark shape of Calhoun's head nodded twice. He was about to plunge the bowie knife into Becker's heart and get it over with, but he stayed his hand.

Calhoun had no sympathy for the billiards parlor owner. But he realized that Becker could very well be lying to him about all this. If that were true, and Calhoun killed him now, Calhoun would have no other leads to follow to find Nichols. If, however, he let Becker live, he could come back and haunt the little man. Besides, he knew he could kill Becker at any time he chose to.

"Best have that ear seen to," Calhoun said without pity. "And I'd not cotton much to it was you to try'n get in my way concernin' any of this."

"I won't say nothin' to nobody," Becker mumbled.

But even as he was speaking, the dark shadow that had been Wade Calhoun had slipped away. Becker heard the door open and shut. He spun, anger beginning to replace the overwhelming fear. His hand gripped the edge of the bar for support.

Becker smelled something putrid, and realized he had soiled his pants. "I'll get you for this, you bastard," he muttered.

Pain flooded back into the side of his head, and he remembered his ear. He dropped to his hands and knees and flapped his hands around frantically trying to find the lost appendage. He finally did.

Cradling the bloody thing in his hands, he raced outside, heading for the physician's office. He hoped Doctor Zargathesey could somehow sew the ear back on.

CHAPTER

* 12 *

Wade Calhoun was aware that half the people of Cimarron were watching him intently as he rode out of town the next morning. But it did not bother him. He glanced at townsfolk as his horse made its lazy way up the street. Virtually all turned away when his eyes swept theirs.

Willy Becker was one of the few who did not look away. His head pounded with a throbbing ache. Doctor Zargathesey had managed to stitch the ear back on, but even Becker knew it would look like hell for the rest of eternity. Becker's resolve to kill Calhoun— or, rather, have him killed— strengthened with each pulsing throb of pain.

But Becker had not said anything of this incident to Sheriff McCloskey, even when the lawman had asked. Becker had just grunted something and walked away, leaving the sheriff wondering. The billiards parlor owner was worried that Calhoun actually would come back and kill him. But he also wanted to take care of it himself, or arrange for it rather than having McCloskey arrest Calhoun. That would never do.

Two others watched with interest as Calhoun rode out of Cimarron: McCloskey, who silently wished Calhoun well, and Amanda Powell.

The young woman watched with a mixture of feelings. Calhoun made her feel weak in the knees and as giddy as a schoolgirl whenever he was around. That annoyed her.

But she also partially accepted those feelings, and she wished he knew about them.

Mostly, though, she still saw him as the man to bring God's, and her own, vengeance to the animals who had treated her mother so brutally. She was not, by nature, a bloodthirsty woman. But this time, she wanted the heads of the seven men.

Calhoun did not see Amanda watching him, nor did he know of her feelings. He would not have cared even if he had known. He had a job at hand, and his entire being was focused on that right now.

There was just a hint of autumn in the damp air as he left Cimarron. The rain had continued off and on throughout the night. It showed signs of doing so today, too. Calhoun huddled in his canvas coat, thankful for the new clothes. He usually cared little for what he wore. But considering the inclement weather, it was a relief to have garments that were not torn, faded and full of holes.

Calhoun rode about due west out of Cimarron. That morning, at breakfast, he had asked Sheriff McCloskey about Cimarron Canyon, wanting to get a little information on the place. He still didn't know much about it, but he knew enough to be able to get there. Once he did that, he could concern himself with finding Nichols and the others.

Just before leaving, he also had gotten wanted posters on the miscreants. He knew none of them by sight, only reputation. The poorly drawn posters would help him identify the outlaws when he found them. And he had no doubt that he would find them sooner or later. He hoped it was sooner. He had found in his experience that swift justice was good justice. That old saw about revenge tasting sweetest when served cold was just so many words, as far as he could tell.

The canyon, he found when he rode into it about midday two days later, was almost a pass. The long saddle of rocky land was five miles long and about two wide. Thick stands of pines and aspens alternated with open, sweeping meadows. Mountainous walls, some precipitous, others more gently sloping, bounded the sides to north and south.

Game—deer, elk, mountain sheep, even a few buffalo—was plentiful. With the Cimarron River flowing swiftly through the canyon fed by numerous streams and creeks, water would not be a problem. And firewood would be easy to find considering the amount of timber. Camps here would be comfortable, Calhoun figured.

Calhoun set up a small base camp in a short finger of a gully that edged off the main canyon. He wasted no time in beginning to explore Cimarron Canyon, looking for sign of the desperadoes.

He found nothing by the time darkness crawled over the land, and he turned the blotchy bay horse toward the camp. His mule, which he had brought to pack in the supplies, waited patiently. Calhoun cared for his horse, cooked and ate his supper, and then turned in.

The next day he went about his explorations in a slow, methodical way. Yet even with all his skill as a tracker, he could find nothing to lead him to Nichols and the six others. If they had been there—and he had no doubt they had—most traces of it were gone. Any traces of which direction they had gone had long ago been washed away by the rains.

He did discover, though, that there were numerous small canyons off the main one. Many would make good hideouts. As would the frequent caves that dotted the mountainsides and palisades.

In some places, he found evidence that the outlaws had been there. In a few, it appeared that the seven men, and possibly more, had spent considerable time. But there were no clues as to where they were now.

Increasingly irritated, Wade Calhoun spent almost a week and a half currycombing the canyon and its many draws, washes, gullies, and aberrations. Still, he found nothing.

By the time he had been over every inch of the Cimarron and its tributaries, Calhoun was in a fine rage. He stomped and kicked about his camp, startling the two animals.

Finally he sat to supper. It was pretty well burned, since he had been so busy raging that he had paid the cooking little attention. Halfway through the meal he decided that he must be presenting quite a picture of himself, even if no one else was around to see him.

He could see a little humor in it. Here he was, an angry young man bolting down chunks of burned elk meat, drinking coffee that was so thick it was almost soupy.

"Shit," he finally muttered aloud. He tossed the burned elk meat out into the darkness. He could hear coyotes fighting over the meat. He put more on the fire, and added a goodly portion of fresh water to the coffee.

He had to admit to himself that the new meal was somewhat better. Especially since he had managed to relax considerably. And with the relaxation came a decision.

It was obvious that the men he was seeking were not in Cimarron Canyon. Therefore, they must be somewhere else. Calhoun decided he would ride out the next morning, heading for Taos. That was the likely place to start looking for them. If they were not there, he might be able to glean some news of them.

He rode out the next morning, moving swiftly. He could see no reason for dawdling. He figured that with a good ride, he could make Taos just after nightfall.

He did better than expected, trotting into the dusty, dirt-brown town an hour before dark. He left the horse and mule in the first livery he spotted. Then he found a hotel and got a room. After a hot, filling supper, he headed for a saloon.

With a bottle of rye in one hand, and the wanted posters in the other, he moved through the saloon, asking everyone if they had seen the outlaws.

No one had. Or so they all said. Calhoun had no reason to doubt them, but it was growing harder to control his temper.

He moved on to another saloon, then another, and still another. As each brought more frustration, Calhoun grew angrier and angrier. But at the fifth tavern, he found a man who had spotted at least two of the killers.

"When?" Calhoun asked curtly.

"Day before yesterday," the grizzled old Mexican replied. He had a thick accent. His eyes lingered on the bottle that sat next to Calhoun's right elbow.

"Where?" Calhoun asked. His voice was a low snarl.

The Mexican licked his lips, never taking his eyes off the bottle.

Calhoun noticed it. He held the bottle out. As the old man reached for it, Calhoun snatched it back just beyond the Mexican's grasp. "Where?"

"Little place called Sierra."

"Where's that?"

"North of here. A day's ride. Maybe less." The accent made him a little hard to understand.

"You sure it was them?"

"*Si.*" The man's eyes never wavered from the bottle.

"Only two of 'em? No more?" Calhoun demanded.

"*Si. Si.*" The man's head bobbed, the worn sombrero doing a little dance atop his head.

"I find out you've been lyin', you old coot, and I'll cut your throat," Calhoun snapped as he handed the Mexican the bottle.

But the old man did not hear him. He was too intent on the half-full bottle that was now in his hands. He smiled, showing several gaps where there once had been teeth.

Calhoun checked with the hotel owner in the morning, asking where Sierra was. He got the same answer the old Mexican had given him. He had been concerned that perhaps the old man had been a drunk and was just making up a story to get the bottle. But at least he had been telling the truth about where the town was. Calhoun could do nothing less than check it out.

The saddle tramp filled up at breakfast. He figured it would keep him from having to stop for a midday meal. He wanted to get to Sierra as quickly as possible. Even if the Mexican had been telling the truth, that had been a couple of days ago now. It would be at least another before he could get there. They could have moved on already.

He might have made the trip by nightfall, but he was forced to hole up for more than three hours as a small band of Apaches roamed through the area.

He had almost walked into their temporary noon-time camp. Only the mule's sudden balkiness had alerted Calhoun that something was out there. Calhoun had pulled off the trail and carefully worked up into the rocks and brush. When he figured he was just about out of earshot, he settled in to wait. He could just barely see the camp.

Calhoun had catnapped some while still trying to keep an eye on the Apaches. They moved out about an hour and a half after Calhoun had arrived. He waited for a good while, still, wanting to make sure the Indians were well away from the area. He had no desire to tangle with a bunch of hardened Apache warriors if he could help it.

Finally, he was on his way again but he had lost considerable time. In late afternoon, he realized he would not be able to make Sierra before dark, and so he slowed his pace. He thought to continue on, even after nightfall had come. Then he decided that was stupid. He did not know the trail or the area. He could easily ride himself off a cliff. He didn't mind so much that he would die, but doing that would leave the miscreants who had ravaged Mother Powell unpunished. He would not allow that to happen because of foolishness.

Just before dark, he pulled into a copse and made his camp. There was little elaborate about it. Within an hour, he was asleep.

In the morning, Calhoun waited only long enough to have enough light to see the trail by. Then he was riding on. He took his time now, giving the animals a little break. He arrived at his destination with the sun almost directly overhead.

The town of Sierra was about what he expected. It was little more than a cluster of poor adobe buildings huddled around a plaza. The plaza was barren except for the town well. The buildings, fewer than a dozen, had seen better days. Their porticos sagged on old poles and torn draperies flapped in the few windows fortunate enough to have such luxuries.

Small dust devils swirled occasionally as Calhoun clomped through the plaza. He headed straight for a building with a gaily painted sign that announced:

CANTINA

Despite the altitude of the wretched little town, the sun was hotter than blazes. It made the town feel like an inferno. Even the numerous dogs could find little energy for barking. Chickens, goats and sheep clustered under trees or brush—any place they could find a little shade from the staggeringly bright sun.

Several of the town's residents were taking *siestas* in the shade. Their sombreros were pulled down over their eyes.

Calhoun stopped in front of the *cantina*. He could hear someone inside playing an ocarina. The player sounded bored. Calhoun dismounted. He pulled the bit from his horse's mouth and let the steed drink lukewarm water from the wooden trough. When the animal had had its fill, Calhoun allowed the mule to drink, too, while he put the bit back in the horse's mouth.

When the mule was done, Calhoun tied both animals to a rickety hitching post. He pulled his hat off and wiped his sweating head with a bandanna and walked inside the *cantina*.

The coolness and dimness of the saloon's interior was something of a shock after the searing heat and brightness of the sun. Calhoun blinked rapidly, trying to clear the film of brightness-induced tears. He felt vulnerable for those few moments before his eyes adjusted to the gloom.

He felt some relief as he realized there were only three other men in the *cantina*, the bartender and two Mexican patrons. Calhoun walked to the bar. "You got rye?" he asked.

"No. Tequila."

Calhoun placed a coin on the bar.

After the bartender had filled his glass and set the bottle down, Calhoun pulled out the wanted fliers. "You seen any of these *hombres* lately?" he asked.

The bartender studied the pieces of paper with rapt attention. It didn't matter to him one way or the other what these damn *gringos* did. He was neither for or against either party in such matters. He finally nodded and pointed a greasy, stubby finger at two pictures.

"Where?"

"*Aqui.* Here."

"When?"

The bartender lifted the blunt finger and aimed it over Calhoun's shoulder.

CHAPTER

* 13 *

Calhoun turned to see two men stepping through the *cantina's* swinging doors. Like Calhoun had done a few minutes earlier, the men stopped and let their eyes adjust to the low light in the windowless saloon.

Calhoun recognized Jaron Cridlow and one of the two men of Nichols's gang for whom names had not been found. He nodded and spun back. "*Gracias,*" he mumbled to the bartender.

In one smooth move, Calhoun scooped up the wanted posters and stuffed them into his shirt pocket. Then he chugged down the shot of tequila in front of him. Once more he turned. He took two steps away from the crude plank bar and stopped.

"Mornin', boys," Calhoun said. Frost nearly dripped from the simple words.

Cridlow and the other man stopped, glaring. Neither said a word, but both moved their hands slowly toward their pistols.

"Mornin'," Cridlow said cautiously. He paused a moment, then asked, "I know you?"

"Nope." Calhoun fought back the impulse to just shoot both men down right off. But he wanted them to know why they were going to die in a moment.

"Didn't think so." Cridlow shifted, moving to his right a little. It put a bit of space between him and his partner.

Calhoun did not mind. He glanced at the two. Cridlow was a thin, blank-faced slob with bad teeth and crossed eyes. The other was young, maybe only seventeen or so. He looked earnest but half-witted. Calhoun felt no sympathy for either.

"Why the greetin', then, pal?" Cridlow asked. He was as cautious as a weasel.

"I always greet the men I'm fixin' to kill directly," Calhoun said simply.

"Shit," Cridlow said with a phlegm-laced laugh. "You hear that, Abe?" he said, apparently to his companion.

"Sure did," the young man said. He had a girl's high-pitched voice.

"And just what did me and Abe here do to bring a buffalo-lovin' bastard like you out like some kind of avengin' angel?" He thought this amusing, in a deadly sort of way.

"You remember an old lady you soiled and then killed over in Cimarron?" Calhoun asked. The words were clipped, as sharp as his finely honed bowie.

"I recall sportin' with some ol' hag over there," Cridlow answered, voice tightening. "But she was willin'." He laughed disgustingly again. "Hell, she was more'n that. She was downright encouragin'. Ain't that right, Abe?"

"Sure was." Abe tried to smile but could not manage it. He felt sick. He thought he was long shed of that episode, considering he and the others had shot hell out of the posse that had followed them. Besides, it had been nearly three weeks since that.

Cridlow's words sent a fine, red film of rage skittering across Calhoun's vision. The saddle tramp burned with hate. In the blink of an eye, one of the Colt Dragoons was in his fist. Almost reflexively, he fired.

Cridlow had no chance to even move as three .44-caliber slugs drilled holes in his chest. Two of the bullets exploded out the back, spraying the room behind him with blood, skin, and fragments of his spine.

Cridlow fell, twisting. He landed in a grotesque heap, the stupid, leering grin never leaving his face.

The young man named Abe never had a chance either.

He stood in stunned awe in the fraction of a second that it took his partner to be shredded. He knew he, too, would be dead in a moment. Frantically he made a futile, eleventh-hour attempt to wrench his pistol out of the hard leather holster.

Abe gasped and his eyes widened as a shock like the kick of a giant mule shattered his gun arm, rendering the limb useless. He heard a scream from far off, and could not recognize that he had made the animalistic sound.

Another blinding blast of pain hit him, and his splintered right leg was blown out from under him. He toppled. There was so much pain from his minced leg and arm that he never felt his nose cracking against the *cantina's* hard-packed dirt floor.

As he lay on the dirt, he was aware of the blood pulsing from the throbbing wounds.

Abe was in intense pain, but conscious. He was

aware of it when Calhoun moved up and knelt beside him. He blinked, wishing the pain would go away. He didn't want to die, but right now he thought death preferable to the agony he was in.

Calhoun could have easily killed both men right off. But a last-minute burst of common sense stayed his death hand. He settled for killing Cridlow, whom Calhoun figured the more dangerous of the two, and wounding the young man named Abe.

It was not a sudden burst of pity that kept him from killing Abe instantly. Instead, it was the realization that he might be able to wring from the seriously wounded young man some information on the other gang members.

Calhoun shoved the empty Dragoon into his holster and pulled the other. He didn't figure he would need it, but he wanted it in hand just in case some damnfool Samaritan came bursting in aiming to cause some mischief. He walked directly and but unhurriedly to Abe's side and knelt.

He ignored Cridlow. Calhoun knew that the outlaw was dead, and he could see no reason for wasting time checking over the body.

"Where's the others, boy?" he asked. His voice held not a single note of compassion.

"It hurts," Abe moaned. "It hurts." He had fouled his pants, and the odor wafted over him. He wrinkled his nose at it. He was embarrassed, despite the agony.

"It's gonna hurt a hell of a lot more you don't answer me, boy," Calhoun warned harshly.

"It hurts." Abe was crying and sobbing and moaning, all at the same time. It made an interesting sound.

"Where're the others, goddamnit?" Calhoun asked in a growling voice.

"What others?" Abe seemed to have regained a little of his senses, though he still sobbed.

"The others that killed Mother Powell."

"Who's she?" The youth seemed blank.

"The kindly woman you debased and then killed over in Cimarron."

Calhoun had a sick feeling in his stomach. The foulness arose whenever he thought of Mother Powell lying there helpless while these animals . . .

He grabbed the young man by the throat and squeezed. "Answer me, goddamnit!"

"Ain't sure," Abe squawked.

Calhoun eased the pressure a little. "I ain't of a mood for joshin', boy," he snapped. "Tell me."

"Garth and two of the others were headin' for Black Water, over east of Taos."

"I just came from east of Taos." Calhoun's tone was menacing. "Through Cimarron Canyon."

"Black Water's south of there a little," Abe gasped. Numbness was creeping over him.

"What about the others?" Calhoun demanded. "There was seven of you bastards in Cimarron."

"Me'n Jaron wasn't of a mind to go along this time." Abe sucked in his breath as a new wave of pain flooded over him. When he opened his eyes again, they were cloudy and dull. "Jaron wanted to come here and see some *señorita* he's been dallyin' with of a time. Said she had a sister for me."

The young man tried to chuckle, but it ended in a paroxysm of pain-racked coughing.

When the fit was over, Abe said, "Warren and Case said they were goin' to one of the pueblos south of Taos. They both had Injun whores they were sportin' with . . ." The words ground to a halt, though moans still burbled past Abe's lips.

"Where're they supposed to meet up?" Calhoun's voice contained a note of urgency. He knew he had little time left. He figured Abe wouldn't live much longer at the rate he was losing blood.

"Cimarron Canyon." Abe's voice was a mere whisper. Life seemed to fade from his eyes and then return.

"When?"

"Eighteenth." Abe's body was racked with spasms and he shook uncontrollably.

Calhoun knew he had learned all he would from the young man. He stood up and turned.

"You should kill him, *señor*," the bartender said. He sounded awed.

"To hell with him."

"He is suffering."

"He don't deserve no better." Calhoun headed for the doors. People had been watching there. They scattered.

As he reached the doors, Calhoun stopped and turned back to face the bartender. "If I hear you've helped him any, you'll suffer his fate, *señor*."

Calhoun shoved through the doors. Dark faces peered at him with fear. He managed to keep the sneer off his face as he climbed into his saddle. He thought for a moment of explaining what these two men had done. Then he decided that these people neither deserved nor needed any explanation.

He turned his horse and slapped it with the reins. It trotted out of Sierra, the mule following placidly behind. They left a small hanging cloud of dust behind them.

Calhoun slowed the horse as he rounded the first bend in the small trail south of Sierra. He was in no real hurry. The outlaws were expected to regroup in Cimarron in three days. He figured that if he traveled steadily, he would make it in about two. That would give him time to set up a small base camp and keep an eye peeled for the desperadoes.

He stopped half a mile on. Watching his back trail, Calhoun reloaded the empty Colt Dragoon without cleaning it first. He did not want to take the time for that now.

With no trouble on the trail, Calhoun made it to Taos just after dark had fallen. He took the same room in the hotel. After supper, he spent an hour in one of the saloons. Then he went back to his room.

Carefully he used a ball puller to extract the round, lead balls from the dirty six-shooter. He poured out the powder. Then he cleaned the weapon well, oiled it, and reloaded it.

When he finished, he wiped himself down with an old cloth and a little water poured in the basin. Then he turned in and slept dreamlessly.

He was on the road an hour after dawn, leisurely riding eastward on the road to Cimarron. Late in the day, he arrived at the mouth of Cimarron Canyon. He decided to stay there rather than trying to find a place inside the canyon that night.

He spotted a trail that angled to the northwest. He

followed it deep into the pine forest until he came to a small, brush-surrounded clearing.

It was evident that the place had been used as a campsite many times. Calhoun shrugged. He figured he might have a little trouble finding firewood, but his need for it was small. He didn't expect that anyone else would be coming along that night. And if they did, he figured he would just have to discourage them from staying here.

A creek bubbled musically over stones nearby. It would provide more than sufficient water for him and his animals. He began making camp.

CHAPTER

* 14 *

Calhoun made his way cautiously into the canyon the next morning to set up his base. He figured that Warren Shoemaker and the outlaw named Case would be coming from behind him. Nichols, Harry Graham, and Conley Muir most likely would be coming through one of the smaller canyons to the south. But Calhoun had no idea which one. He didn't expect them to come up the road that was marked for Black Water.

He could not divine what they were going to do. He would just have to do what he could to lessen the odds of them slipping by him. He pressed on, moving a little more quickly.

Calhoun did take the time, though, to stop and shoot a good-size female elk. As he gutted and bled the animal, he thought of fresh elk steak for supper. It was a pleasing thought.

About halfway through the canyon, he pulled into a ravine that angled sharply off on the north side. It was a well-watered gully, with steep, rocky walls that were barren of vegetation. Giant boulders lay about, and a trickle of a creek ran through it. He found a spot sheltered by some cottonwoods and pines.

Calhoun unpacked the mule and turned it out to

graze on the deep, browning grass. Then he unsaddled the horse. After currying the animal, he turned it out to graze.

Working methodically, Calhoun gathered a decent pile of firewood and kindling. In a hollow dugout of the canyon wall by a long-ago flood, he built a fire.

When the blaze was going well, he stepped back as far as he could and watched, then nodded in satisfaction. The smoke, filtered through the tree branches and leaves, and half-stopped by a rocky overhang, would not be visible for much distance. Calhoun went back to the fire, set the coffeepot on and then cooked up some beans while roasting several chunks of the elk meat.

He ate a leisurely meal, and followed it with a cigarette and cup of coffee. Then he pulled his rifle from the saddle scabbard and the collapsing telescope he had bought in Cimarron from one of his saddlebags. After a moment's hesitation, he delved back into his saddlebags and grabbed one of the three pint bottles of rye whiskey he had bought in Taos.

He stuffed the whiskey and telescope into his shirt. Then he began climbing the slightly sloped canyon wall. It was laborious work, and soon he was sweating. He paused when he could to wipe the perspiration away with a bandanna.

It took almost an hour, but he finally made it to the rock ledge above his fire. He stood there, breathing hard and looking around. He had a view of three directions, but the fourth was blocked by the canyon wall.

Calhoun spotted another ledge ten feet above him. He hoped it was the lip of this small canyon.

After a short rest, he clambered up the rest of the way and soon found himself standing on a promontory at the top of the canyon. The rim was only six feet wide at this point. Calhoun checked and saw another canyon wall falling away on the west side. While the cliff separating the two canyons was only six feet wide at the top here, it was considerably thicker at the bottom. Neither canyon wall was perpendicular; each sloped outward from the top.

The rim also narrowed to a point a few feet from where he stood. The point faced south.

His canyon headed off northeast, and the other one went northwest. The flat top widened as it moved away from the promontory. But it also dipped some. Calhoun figured he had the best spot right where he was.

A lonely piñon pine stood bravely on the rocky, uneven promontory. The heat was fierce, but the wind whistled along at a good clip.

Calhoun sat cross-legged near the tree. There were too many branches too low for Calhoun to be able to lean against it, but the piñon served as something of a wind break. He set the rifle down on the rock near his right knee.

After his breathing had gone back to normal, Calhoun pulled out the telescope, extended it—and took a long, slow look around. He saw nothing out of the ordinary, though he was fascinated by the soft, superb gliding of a huge golden eagle. The big bird soared on the currents, hardly beating a wing. Calhoun envied the bird more than a little.

Long training kept Calhoun from being dulled by

the boredom that crept over him. He didn't understand quite how he did it, but he managed to keep alert yet at the same time rest. Anyone watching him would have thought him almost asleep. Or at least daydreaming. He might have been, but he still was aware of all that went on around him.

Throughout the rest of the long day, he sipped from his small bottle of rye, and puffed on cigarettes. Every half-hour, he would put the telescope to his eye and make a slow, careful scan in all directions.

He saw nothing.

As dusk began lowering, he stood, yawned and stretched. His thoughts drifted to Lizbeth, but he clamped his mind shut on such thoughts. Instead, he let his mind wander over the possibilities offered by Amanda Powell. He had been in such a rage at Mother Powell's murder and the brutality of it, he had paid little attention to Mother Powell's daughter.

He had, of course, noted that she was more than attractive. She was downright beautiful. Her figure was built for giving pleasure. She had her mother's sauciness, and like her mother, never offended with it.

Calhoun knew that Amanda was not a woman any man would ever run roughshod over. She was no meek little mouse who would rush to do a man's bidding whenever he asked. Calhoun suspected that any man would have a handful of trouble should he take it into his mind to start issuing orders to the beautiful Miss Amanda Powell.

Calhoun also suspected, though, that if Amanda ever gave her heart to a man, she would give it wholly, without reserve. He thought she would do the same with her body.

Calhoun grinned tightly. While he might want to explore the plush treasures Amanda offered, he was equally certain he would not want to get too tangled up with her. He was not the type of man to settle down. He had found that out with Lizbeth. He needed plenty of free rein. He needed the freedom to roam. Amanda might allow him such independence, but she would not like it, and would be hurt by it. She was strong-willed enough not to stand it for too long.

He thrust the thoughts of Amanda and her well-rounded figure out of his mind. For now. He decided that he would stop back in Cimarron after all this was over and see if Miss Amanda Powell might be willing to thank him in a most pleasurable way.

Until then, though, he thought sourly, he had best keep his mind on business.

Calhoun swallowed the last sip of whiskey and sent the bottle flying, twirling out over the point of the promontory. It twinkled a moment in the dying glow of the sun before disappearing from sight. A few seconds later, Calhoun heard the bottle crash on the rocks far below.

He stuffed the telescope back into his shirt and then began the arduous climb down the steep face of the canyon wall. Heading down was easier than getting up, but it still took a while and it was dark when Calhoun's feet finally touched terra firma.

After catching his breath, Calhoun stoked up the fire. He sliced off a good-size steak from the elk and dangled it by a green stick over the low flames. He was sick of beans, so he made up a batch of biscuits.

He took his time eating. Afterward, he had several

cigarettes and two cups of coffee.

As he sat, he honed his bowie. His father had given him the knife when Calhoun was seventeen and ready to strike out on his own. Calhoun cherished it. Not so much because his father had given it to him, but more because it was a fine weapon. The workmanship on the blade was superb, and the deer antler handle was fitted perfectly to his hand after so many years of use.

Calhoun checked on the horse and mule, made water, and then spread out his bedroll. He lay down and was asleep almost instantly.

He spent the next two days on his perch high atop the canyon. Throughout the first full day, he managed to keep his temper in check. But as dusk began moving in on the second full day, he began to curse quietly and steadily. He was certain now that young Abe had lied through his teeth despite being at death's door.

Calhoun climbed down and began making his supper. The elk meat was almost bad now because of the heat. Calhoun figured he would get this one more meal out of the elk. In the morning, he would get rid of the rest of the carcass. The more rancid the meat got, the more it would attract scavengers. All he needed, he thought, was a pack of hungry wolves or a grizzly bear moving in on him.

He figured he would decide in the morning whether he would do some hunting. He had spent all the daylight hours of the past two and a half days up on the promontory. He might have no fresh meat, but he did have plenty of bacon, beans, salt beef, and flour left. That would hold him for several more days at least.

He would also have to decide what to do about trying to find the outlaws. If Abe had lied to him, the killers might not be back through this canyon for days or weeks. If he wasn't lying—Calhoun admitted Abe might have just gotten his dates messed up—they could be along at any time. Calhoun thought the latter more likely, considering how half-witted Abe had been.

Calhoun was as comfortable as could be expected here in this campsite. He would hate to pull up stakes for no good reason. He sighed and tossed his cigarette butt into the fading fire. *Tomorrow*, he thought. *Tomorrow, I'll make all those decisions.*

In the morning, all his indecision was gone. He made up his mind while he was gobbling down hot chunks of fatty bacon and slurping up coffee. He would head for Black Water. If he couldn't find Nichols or any of the outlaw's cronies there, he might be able to pick up their trail. After that, he would see what happened.

A sense of serenity surrounded him now that he had decided on a course of action. He was in no hurry really, so he dawdled over another cup of coffee.

Climbing the cliff again, he took one final look around through the telescope. He spotted a cloud of dust on the eastern horizon, and his heart quickened. He watched for the better part of an hour before he realized it was only a small wagon train moving along the trail toward Cimarron.

"Damn," he muttered. He realized he was disappointed that his mission was not to reach a climax yet. Then he shrugged.

Calhoun slid and climbed back down the mountain.

By the time he had packed his supplies and saddled his horse, it was midmorning. He rode out, heading west.

He left the canyon and late in the day, some miles later, he found a sign at the fork of the main trail to Taos and a smaller one that ran off into the pines to the south. The sign was a simple one, just some flat blue paint on a plain pine board: Black Water 11 miles.

Since it was so close to dark, Calhoun decided to make camp. He could be in Black Water before noon tomorrow. He heard the rush of a brook off to the east a little. He forced the bay horse through some brush toward the sound. He found a spot bare of brush in an area barely large enough to spread his bedroll. It would suffice.

Calhoun had a cold meal of elk jerky brought from Cimarron and water from the cold brook. It wasn't the best meal he had ever had, but it was far better than others. He was content enough with it.

After eating, he pushed into the bushes to relieve himself. As he was cleaning himself up afterward, the wind shifted. It brought a momentary silence to the area around him, deadening the sound of the brook.

Into the gap floated voices.

CHAPTER

* 15 *

Like a shadow, Calhoun moved back to his camp. The mule clomped a foot and the horse snuffled. As soon as the animals realized who was approaching, they quieted. Calhoun patted both on the neck.

Calhoun silently pulled the Greener shotgun from the saddle scabbard. He hastily checked both charges in the light of the half moon. As he closed the weapon, he muffled the sound against his body.

Then he moved off, heading north. He had heard the sounds west of him, but he wanted to come up on whoever it was from a direction they might not expect.

There was a good chance, he knew, that the voices he had heard were from a bunch of innocent travelers. But he had to be sure and he had to be alert. He hoped the men were with Nichols, all of them together. If they were, he would be able to end all this right here and now.

Calhoun moved stealthily through the night. He froze every time his foot snapped a twig. After a few moments, he would move on again, fairly certain that he had not been detected.

It took more than two hours for Calhoun to make his way a half-mile north, cross the Black Water road, and make his way toward the other camp. He came in slowly, from the west, hoping to throw them off.

As he neared the camp, he heard the voices again. He could distinguish no words, but he could detect only two different voices. He was somewhat disappointed. If it was Nichols' men in the camp, there were only two of them. That meant he would still have to find the others after a while.

But first things first, he decided. It was most important to find out just who these two men were. If they were of the outlaw band, he would take care of them. Then, and only then, would he worry about finding the rest of the desperadoes.

He edged up toward the camp. He scarcely breathed. He moved only inches at a time, wanting to risk no sound whatsoever. Then he was peering through the foliage at the camp.

One man sat quietly at the fire. He was puffing on a cigar and swilling whiskey from a big bottle. In the firelight, Calhoun could see that it was Warren Shoemaker.

Dimly in the background, out of the circle of light, Calhoun saw a bedroll and a huddled mass. Calhoun nodded. The second man must have turned in just minutes ago. If one of the men were asleep, his job would be all the easier.

Once again, Calhoun knew he should just gun these two villains down from where he was. But he wanted them to be sure they knew why they were dying.

He pushed out from the brush and in half a dozen steps was in the light.

Shoemaker looked up startled, then covered it well.

"Welcome, stranger," he said evenly. He pointed his coffee cup at Calhoun. "Coffee's hot. And you don't need that damned scattergun to help yourself to the pot."

Shoemaker was a rather handsome man, with a glib manner. Only the tic in his right eye, and the thin line of drool that constantly dribbled out of the one corner of his mouth gave any indication that he was a psychopath.

"Piss in your coffee," Calhoun snarled.

Shoemaker looked up at Calhoun again. Anger smoldered in Shoemaker's eyes. He had no idea who this cocky, shotgun-toting man was, but he sure as hell did not take kindly to being spoken to in such a way by any man. "You got some kind of beef here, mister?" he asked cautiously.

"You've got to answer for the soiling and murder of Mother Powell. Both you and your partner there." Calhoun jerked his head in the direction of the bedroll.

Shoemaker managed to keep the sudden elation he felt out of his eyes and voice. He figured he and his new partner, Case Whitson, had this hard-eyed wild man dead to rights now. All he had to do was keep Calhoun distracted just a few moments longer.

"I got no idea what the hell you're talkin' about, mister," Shoemaker said calmly.

Calhoun shrugged. "Then you'll go to hell a liar as well as a killer."

"I ain't killed nobody." The twitch in his eye became more pronounced. It always did when the urge — and opportunity — to kill someone arose.

Calhoun shrugged again, unconcerned. "Lyin' to

save your miserable ass ain't very becomin'," Calhoun commented. "But if you want to leave this earth with a lie on your lips, beggin' for your life, that's your account."

Something nagged at Calhoun's brain. There was something not right here. He knew he was missing something, probably something vital. But he could not pin it down.

Shoemaker watched as Calhoun's thumb snapped back both hammers of the scattergun. Shoemaker tensed. "Now, Case!" he roared. He flung the cup of coffee at Calhoun even as he shoved off the log, falling to his right. At the same time, his right hand darted for his Colt pistol.

Several things became apparent to Calhoun in the blink of an eye. One was that there was no one in the bedroll, that it most likely was a pile of gear. Another was that he was in deep trouble.

But he was a man accustomed to dealing with the most urgent problem first. He fired both barrels of the shotgun. The roar was deafening, even in the open like this.

Both loads of buckshot tore into Shoemaker. They left the upper right side of his chest, the side of his neck and half his face in tatters. Shoemaker, who had been moving, landed with a plop in the dirt, pistol only halfway out of his holster. He lay, his arms and legs twitching as disrupted, destroyed nerves tried in vain to work properly.

Calhoun threw down the scattergun. He was pulling one of Dragoons, swirling at the same time, when he felt the icy fire of a bullet rip into his back. He felt his legs buckle and he started to go down.

"Damn, son of a bitch," he whispered.

Another heavy pistol ball crashed into the upper portion of his shoulder, knocking him flat down onto his face. He groaned involuntarily.

Calhoun had dropped the one Dragoon when he was shot the first time. He managed to push himself up on his arms and then roll over onto his back. Twisting his hand backward, he pulled the Dragoon from the holster on his right side. A bullet kicked up dirt an inch from his head.

Ignoring the searing agony that lanced through him, Calhoun rolled twice more, until he ran into the log on which Shoemaker had been sitting. In his rolling, he had seen a muzzle flash. The bullet had missed him, but not by much.

With a massive force of will, Calhoun brought himself up into a sitting position. The Dragoon snapped up at the end of his arm. "Your dumb ass is mine now, you lady-murderin' son of a bitch," he muttered in rage.

Another muzzle flash burst from the brush. Calhoun had no idea where the ball went. He simply fired four times at where the shot had come from.

There was a crashing in the brush, like a man staggering. One final crash, like a body falling. And then silence.

Calhoun realized at last where the final bullet fired at him had gone. He felt a burning across his left side and knew the ball had sliced him. That one, he noted, was the least of his worries.

The first wound was the worst. That ball had hit

him low in the back and blew out through the front. Blood still gushed from the exit wound; he could not be sure how bad it was in the back. But he had seen other men shot similarly, and he feared he had suffered damage to some vital organs.

"So," he muttered, "are you just gonna sit here on your ass and die?" He spit in self-anger. After holstering the Dragoon, he slid on his behind — using his one good arm and his legs for power — to the pile of gear near the bedroll. He found an old shirt and a lady's chemise. From one of Shoemaker's conquests, Calhoun figured. He cut both garments into strips.

Making another mighty effort, he managed to squiggle over to the fire. He stuck the blade of his bowie knife into the embers and waited.

When the blade glowed cherry red, Calhoun pulled it free. Without hesitation — with delay would come fear, he knew — he slapped the hot steel against his belly wound.

He sucked in his breath as his skin sizzled. "Shit," he groaned. The smell of burning flesh tickled his nostrils.

Calhoun never did figure out how it was he kept from passing out. But he managed to heat the bowie and cauterize the back wound and both sides of the shoulder wound.

Once that was done, he sat there moaning low in his throat, hoping the agony would ease even a little. He sucked in breath after breath, thinking that might help. But it didn't. The pain remained throbbing and pulsing, as if it had a life of its own.

Calhoun had no idea how long he sat there. But he

finally forced himself into action. As well as he could, he wrapped the strips of bandaging around his wounds. It was a poor job, he knew. But he thought it might keep some of the dirt out of the injuries.

He crawled and squirmed toward the brush. He found the body of a young man. Case Whitson was handsome even in death. Calhoun spit on Whitson's forehead.

It seemed to take forever, but Calhoun crawled over, retrieved his other Colt and the shotgun. He continued moving, and after an eternity, he had made it back to his own camp. His mind seemed to have blocked out the pain. It allowed him to make a weak soup of jerky boiled in canteen water. Calhoun slurped it down hungrily.

He fell asleep several times, but kept snapping awake. He sweated every time, worried about how long he had been out. He was certain that if he fell asleep for real, he would never awaken. But he decided that each time he had dozed off, it had only been for a few minutes.

Dawn began edging into his campsite, surprising him a little. But Calhoun found renewed hope in the light of the fresh day. Even if the pain had returned with a vengeance.

Calhoun knew he had to get help or he would die. But the thought of riding ten or twenty miles to Cimarron was not comforting. He thought he might be a shade closer to Taos. But he knew no one there. He could get the help he needed in Cimarron. He figured that Amanda Powell would watch over him if no one else did.

Calhoun sat looking around his camp. He had a dilemma. He could never get onto his horse without the help of stirrups and such. But he figured he could never get the saddle on the horse in his condition.

A large rock nearby offered the opportunity of perhaps helping him get on the horse. But the saddle was his pride and joy. It was the only decent possession he had. Besides, he could not afford to lose the rifle, shotgun and two Walker pistols, as well as the things he had in his saddlebags.

He sat and watched the sun continue to rise. He was of no mind to make a decision. The pain was unbearable, though he bore it as stoically as he could.

"Shit," he cursed at himself, angry. "If you're gonna die from all this, you might as well be doin' something."

Calhoun closed his eyes a moment, focusing his strength and will. Then he opened his eyes and pushed himself up. The world spun wickedly, and spots flickered before his vision. He leaned back against a tree trunk, grateful that it was there.

After a few moments, Calhoun felt ready to try again. He shuffled forward, an inch or two at a time. But he was making progress.

Picking up the saddle blanket was a little tricky, but tossing it on the bay was easy. The real problem was the saddle. It was heavy under the best of conditions. Calhoun stared at it for some minutes. Then he spit in self-disgust.

"Hell," he muttered. He took a deep breath and grabbed the saddlehorn in one hand and the cantle in the other. He let his breath out in a whoosh and jerked upward.

Calhoun thought for a moment that his insides had exploded. Fire lanced out in all directions, until he felt like his whole body was aflame. But he was moving, his body reacting even as his mind tried to tell him he couldn't.

Calhoun stood gasping, leaning against the nervous horse. The saddle was on the steed's back. It took more than a half-hour of struggle and rest, effort and pain-racked pause, but he managed to tighten the saddle.

After a short, well-deserved rest, Calhoun maneuvered the horse over to the rock. He jammed the bit in its mouth and slipped the bridle over the horse's head. Then he climbed on the rock, stuck a boot in a stirrup and pulled.

A clinging fog of blackness floated before him. When it cleared, Calhoun realized that he was astride the horse. He was weaving, but mounted.

"I hope you know your way home, you goddamn nag," Calhoun said. He touched his heels to the horse's sides. The animal moved out slowly. The mule followed dumbly along in its wake.

Calhoun turned the steed's head north on the Black Water trail, and then east on the main road to Cimarron. Then he slumped and let the horse have its head.

C H A P T E R

* 16 *

Calhoun never really knew when he got into Cimarron. By the time he reached the town, he was delirious. He was bent almost double in the saddle, but he was still on the horse.

The animal, with the mule still plodding peaceably behind, walked into town. The bay went straight to the livery and stopped, waiting patiently for its rider to dismount. It pawed the ground, snuffling and snorting. The mule also stopped and stuck its head between the rails of the corral to reach the pile of hay.

Horatio Smith, who owned the livery stable, came out of the barn, wiping his hands on an old piece of cloth. He glanced at the sky. Dark would be upon them soon, and he looked forward to getting home and having his supper.

Then he spotted the horse he had sold to Amanda Powell a couple of weeks ago for that Mister Calhoun. "Lord," he whispered as he spotted the drooping figure atop the horse. He hurried over to the animal.

It took him only a moment to assess the situation. No genius was needed to take in the slumped man coated with blood and deduce the immediate problem.

"Henry!" Smith called.

A nine-year-old boy popped his head out of the barn door. "Yessir, Pa?"

"Fetch up Sheriff McCloskey. And Doc Zargathesey. Hurry, boy.'"

Henry Smith saw the ghastly man slouched on the blotchy bay horse, and it unnerved him a little. In a town like Cimarron, he had seen blood and death before. But something abut this forlorn, blood-soaked figure chilled him. He raced off, heading off down First Street toward Main Street.

As soon as his son had run off, Horatio Smith moved slowly up to the horse. "Mister Calhoun?" he called softly.

Calhoun's only response was to groan and mumble incoherently.

"Damn," Smith said quietly. He took the reins and tied the horse to the top rail of the corral. He tried pulling Calhoun gently from the saddle, but Calhoun's hands were clamped on the pommel like vises. It took Smith the better part of a quarter-hour to pry the saddle tramp's hands off the saddle horn. Once he had done that, it was but moments before he tugged Calhoun from the saddle.

McCloskey and Zargathesey ran up, led by Henry, just as Smith was easing Calhoun's inert form onto the dirt. He looked up at the physician and lawman. He had seen dead men before, and Wade Calhoun sure as hell looked about ready for a coffin to him.

Zargathesey knelt, sitting on his shins. He tugged off his coat, wrapped it into a rough pillow and stuck it under Calhoun's head. Then he reached into his pocket and pulled out a folding knife. After opening it, he cut off the crude bandages and then slit through the blood-caked rag that had been Calhoun's shirt, exposing the thin, broad chest.

"Good Lord in heaven," Zargathesey breathed.

"He's dead, ain't he, Doc?" Smith asked, sounding somewhat in awe.

Zargathesey shook his head. "I think I can save him," he announced.

"Then what. . . ?" McCloskey asked, confused at the physician's exclamation.

"Well, I've seen men in worse shape than this," Zargathesey allowed as he began looking over the cauterized wounds. His gnarled fingers touched softly here, prodded gently there. "But not many. What really amazes me, though, is that he's still alive after all this time."

The doctor lifted each of Calhoun's eyelids and looked into the dull, lusterless eyes. He mumbled softly as he made his cursory examination.

"How long's it been?" Smith asked.

Zargathesey looked up at the liveryman, his bushy white eyebrows wriggling like hairy caterpillars. "Judging by the way the blood's dried and the skin and all, he must've been wounded sometime late yesterday. Maybe last night. I have no idea how far he's traveled, but he must've come a fair piece."

He shook his head again. "Help me up, you two," he ordered. He held up his arms, crooked at the elbow.

McCloskey and Smith each grabbed him under an armpit and lifted. Once on his feet, the grizzled, fierce-looking physician said, "Ain't a damn thing I can do for him here. Especially with the light failing. Get him to my office."

"You sure you can save him, Doc?" McCloskey asked. He was worried. He sort of liked the saddle tramp, if only because Calhoun had saved his life. But more importantly, he wanted to hear how Calhoun had fared in his mission of vengeance.

"Yep." Zargathesey paused a heartbeat. "If y'all can get him over to my office before winter sets in," he added sarcastically.

"Right." McCloskey looked at Smith. He was suddenly pushed by urgency. "Hitch up a cart, Horatio. *Pronto*."

"It's done," Henry Smith said. The boy walked quickly up, towing a Shetland pony hitched to a small wagon.

Smith nodded at his son. He was proud of the boy, but he was not one to let it show in front of others.

"Well, if you ain't somethin', boy," McCloskey commented favorably. "Come on, Horatio, let's get Mister Calhoun loaded."

It was but a moment's work before the two men had piled Calhoun's groaning body into the small cart. The saddle tramp's legs dangled off the back. Calhoun's boot heels dragged along in the dirt as the odd procession made its way as rapidly as possible toward Doctor Zargathesey's office.

After McCloskey and Smith had carried Calhoun into the examining room, the sheriff said, "On your way back, would you stop by and tell Miss Powell what's happened here?"

"Sure thing, Sheriff." Smith and his son left. The boy

headed with the cart and pony back toward the stable; his father went toward the restaurant.

McCloskey was sitting in a corner, puffing a cigar, relaxing with his head back and feet up on the doctor's table, when Amanda burst into the examining room. Neither the physician, nor his assistant, Vladimir Pavel, looked up from their work over Calhoun when she did.

The young woman had been in a panic in the few minutes since Horatio Smith had come to the restaurant and told her that Wade Calhoun was hurt bad and being tended by Doc Zargathesey. She had torn off her apron, brushed crumbs off her dress, shouted a few orders at her assistant and Melba. Then she had raced pell-mell for the door and the doctor's office.

Amanda gasped in horror as she saw Calhoun. The saddle tramp's bare chest and stomach were bloody, as were Zargathesey's and Pavel's hands. The physician worked, clucking to himself, cutting here, slicing there, probing here, prodding there. He made an occasional quiet comment to Pavel.

"Sit down, Miss Amanda," Zargathesey ordered after a few moments. "I can't work with you hovering over me like some sort of *loco* mother hen."

"But he . . ."

"He'll be fine, I think," Zargathesey said. He straightened momentarily, looking at Amanda. "He's young, stronger than any man I've ever seen, and appears to be determined to live. He'll make it—if you give me the space to do what's necessary."

"Yessir," Amanda said meekly. She took a chair in a corner diagonal to Sheriff McCloskey. She sat, wring-ing her hands, keeping her eyes glued to the surgeon and his work.

Finally Zargathesey stood back as Pavel spread some salves over Calhoun's wounds. With Pavel holding Calhoun's unconscious form up, Zargathesey wrapped clean linen bandages around him. Then Pavel gently settled Calhoun back onto the examining table.

Amanda bit her lips, tense, as Zargathesey and Pavel washed up in a basin. The doctor began rolling down his shirt sleeves as he walked toward Amanda. Pavel grabbed his black frock coat and left the room through a curtained partition.

"Well?" Amanda demanded as the doctor stopped in front of her. She was impatient.

"As I told you before, Miss Powell, he is strong and determined. I see no reason why he should not live a long and healthy life." He did not add that such a statement would be true only if Calhoun gave up his tendency for gunplay.

Amanda nodded. She was not one to fret for long. The doctor had done what he could. The rest, she figured, was up to Wade Calhoun. And if she were the kind of woman to wager, she would place her money on Calhoun. She stood. "Is there anything I can do, Doctor?" she asked.

Zargathesey took in the determined set of Amanda's mouth and jaw. He wished he were thirty years younger. He would give any man in Cimarron a run for his money in the pursuit of this fine young woman. She would be a prize catch for some very lucky man.

"No, Miss Amanda," he answered, sad because of

lost opportunity. But not too sad. Beth Zargathesey might be past her prime, but she was still a fine, helpful woman, and Zargathesey was not disappointed in still being married to her after forty-six years.

"Do you mind if I look in on him now and again?" Amanda asked.

"Now and again?" Zargathesey questioned, thick, white eyebrows raised. He chuckled softly.

Amanda flushed but said nothing.

"No need for embarrassment, miss," Zargathesey said with another chuckle. "I expect your visits'd only do him some good. I know they would me."

Amanda smiled, relieved. "Thank you, Doctor."

"My pleasure, miss." Zargathesey bowed stiffly at the waist.

Amanda nodded once more and left.

Zargathesey watched with interest as she sashayed away into the night. He suddenly realized that Amanda Powell reminded him very much of a young Beth Zargathesey, nee Crocker. He supposed that was why he liked Amanda so much. He turned to face McCloskey.

The lawman was also watching Amanda. His thoughts were, however, more urgently lustful than the old doctor's. As Amanda moved out of the light cast by the street lanterns, McCloskey tore his gaze away. He smiled wanly at the doctor.

Zargathesey nodded at the sheriff. He knew what McCloskey had been thinking, and could understand it. But he also knew that McCloskey had about as much chance of reeling in Amanda Powell as the old doctor had of waking up tomorrow twenty-one years old.

"Help me get him into the other room, Sheriff," Zargathesey said, pointing to Calhoun.

The two men lugged Calhoun into the next room. It was nineteen feet long and perhaps fifteen wide. There were four cots along each wall, facing toward the middle of the room. That left an aisle three feet wide down the center. There was three feet of space between every bed too, giving each patient a minimum of privacy.

The doctor and lawman set Calhoun gently down on the cot nearest the examining room door. Calhoun almost had the room to himself. Only one other bed was occupied—a six-year-old had a case of measles and was sleeping quietly at the far end of the room.

"You really think he's gonna make it, Doc?" McCloskey asked as he and the physician walked back into the examining room. The sheriff suspected that Zargathesey might have been painting a rosy picture of Calhoun's chances for Amanda.

"Yes," Zargathesey said calmly. He meant it. He had seen some men wounded as badly as this during the Mexican War, and even way back in the War of 1812. Some had survived; others had not. He had noted somewhere along the years that the ones who had lived were ones like this saddle tramp here: tough, resolute, with a core of steel and a will that kept driving them no matter the odds.

McCloskey was still not sure he believed the doctor, but he had to take Zargathesey at his word. He nodded. "I'll look in on him when I can, Doc," he said.

"Fine." Zargathesey seemed disinterested. Or distracted.

"If he wakes, send someone for me," McCloskey ordered. "No matter what time of day it is."

"Fine." Zargathesey was thinking about Calhoun, going over in his mind everything he had done for the saddle tramp to save his life. He was barely aware that the sheriff had left. Zargathesey finally decided that there was no more he could have done for Calhoun. He rose and headed for his own rooms.

CHAPTER

* 17 *

Wade Calhoun had trouble waking up. It seemed as if he were fighting through a thick, black cloud that tightly enveloped him. He felt like he would be smothered by it. He desperately wanted light and fresh air.

Panicking a little, he clawed at the clinging wrapper that threatened his existence. He felt his throat spasm as it fought for life-giving air. Strange noises filtered down through the black fog. To him, it sounded like a wounded grizzly bear singing some odd death chant.

He was determined not to give up, though now he began to suspect that he was in a coffin that had been lowered in to the ground. The coffin had no top, but the gravediggers had shoveled in tons of rich, heavy, black dirt over him. He scratched at the clay-like soil, which filled his nose and mouth, shutting off his air. His actions became more frantic.

Amanda dozed in a chair next to Calhoun's bed. One of her hands rested lightly on his forearm nearest her. She had hoped that she might be able to give him some of her strength.

She was worried about Calhoun. Her concern had increased considerably in the two weeks since he had made it back into Cimarron, half-dead. He had shown no signs of waking, though he had been through several bouts of delirium. Those frightened Amanda the most. He thrashed and writhed and shouted words that were so garbled she often could not understand them.

At other times, he spoke in a voice that was virtually normal, except for the mental pain and the anger. He had talked of people named Lizbeth and Lottie, and of Sioux Indians; of Tennessee and Kansas Territory and other places.

None of it made any sense to Amanda, but she did not care. As long as he was making some kind of sound, she held hope in her heart that he would come out of his stupor soon.

During those spells, Amanda would hold Calhoun's hand or wipe his fevered forehead with a cool cloth. She would talk softly to him, saying nothing in particular, but feeling foolish. She would use her considerable strength to try to hold him down when his convulsive jerking worsened. She would try to soothe him with words and soft strokes on his arm or face.

Amanda worried that all her efforts were doing him no good. But she continued them, holding out the hope that maybe she was getting through to him somehow, letting him know that someone was there and cared for him.

The young woman came three or four times a day for the first few days. Then the frequency of her visits increased until she was there virtually round the clock. Like now, she dozed and catnapped when she could, sitting in a chair right next to Calhoun's bed.

That way she would be as close as possible to him.

Amanda had yet to sort out her thoughts about and feelings for Wade Calhoun. She knew she cared for him, but she was not sure how deeply.

She sometimes thought that she cared for him too much but would not admit it to herself.

At other times, she thought she stayed at his side simply because he was the instrument of vengeance for her mother's debasement and death.

At last she finally decided that this was not the time to try to sort such things out. She would wait until he recovered. Then she would see how successful he had been in his mission. After that job was done for Calhoun, she would worry about what she felt for him. That would be time enough.

Amanda snapped awake as the first notes of the scream banged off the walls and assaulted her ears. Her eyes popped open and she jerked upright in the chair. Her heart was slamming in her chest. Fear clawed at her insides.

She looked at Calhoun in surprise. He had not moved at all earlier. Not even a twitch. She would have felt it with her hand on his arm.

Now he was sitting up, sweat pouring down his whiskered face. His eyes looked blank, almost frightened. A slither of drool curled out of the near corner of his mouth. His chest was heaving, as if he had just been through some vast exertion.

"Wade?" Amanda called softly. She wanted him to acknowledge her, but she was afraid that she might startle him. She wasn't sure what would happen if she did that. She was certain she didn't want to find out.

"Wade?" she tried again after getting no response the first time. She waited with bated breath, hoping for a reaction. At this point, she thought, any reaction at all would be good.

There was nothing for some moments. It seemed an eon, but then Calhoun's head slowly swiveled toward her. The eyes looked at her without recognition or animation.

Amanda's heart froze with fear. The wounds and loss of blood must have damaged his mind, she thought.

Then Calhoun blinked, the eyes staying closed for what seemed like an eternity. When they reopened, they sparkled with life, if not humor.

Amanda smiled as relief swelled up out of her heart and spread throughout her body. Her relief was complete when Calhoun smiled weakly back at her.

Calhoun's eyes opened, and the world was spread before him. He had no idea of where he was. He knew it was somehow familiar, and of the world he knew, not of the afterworld.

It took a few minutes for his eyes to focus, and for him to realize that the black envelope of death had been merely a nightmare. He was alive, if not well.

Calhoun heard someone calling his name, and he turned his head toward the sound. He could not recognize the pretty, frightened young woman sitting in the chair next to the bed. He shut his eyes for a moment and took a deep breath.

When he opened his eyes again, he was pleased at the sight of Amanda Powell. He wondered how long she had been there. She seemed more relieved now than frightened. She smiled. He tried to smile back at her, but was not sure how successful he was at it.

The pain in his torso was incredible. He had been shot before, but never so badly as this. He wanted to scream with the intensity of the agony, but he refused to allow that.

He suspected that the scream he had heard just before awakening came from him. But he was not sure. He assuaged his conscience by telling himself that even if it had come from him, it was involuntary and that he had had no control over it.

Amanda was saying something else to him, and he nodded. He had not understood what she had said. The pain had blocked recognition of the words.

Amanda evidently figured he did understand, though. She arose and glanced at him. The look was a mingling of worry and friendliness. Then she headed for the door.

Calhoun breathed in deeply and the fires of hell burned paths across his chest, stomach, back, and shoulders. The blackness wavered anew before his eyes. Rather than let unconsciousness overtake him again, he lay back down. "Shit," he whispered.

The pain eased a little and he found he could breathe normally without feeling like he had an anvil or two sitting on his chest. He acknowledged that the agony was still stunningly intense. But he could bear it, he figured. He would have to, he knew, since there was little that could be done for it.

Except to get roaring drunk and let the alcohol deaden the pain. The thought appealed to him at the moment.

So did the thought of perhaps dying. Soon. Calhoun figured death would be blissful relief from the agony he was in. He almost smiled at that. He was too hard-headed to bring it about by himself, and he figured his body was too stubborn to give up just yet.

Amanda entered the room. Doctor Zargathesey followed her. The physician stopped at the side of the bed and looked down at him. "You look like hell," Zargathesey pronounced as he set his small black bag on the bed.

Amanda gasped at the physician's lack of tact.

"Feel like it, too," Calhoun grunted.

"Well, now that we're straight on all that, let's have a look at you." The doctor opened up his bag and then bent over Calhoun.

Zargathesey peeled away the bandages and looked at the wounds. He said nothing during the examination. Finally he put a fresh layer of salve on the wounds and rebandaged Calhoun.

"All things considered, you seem in good shape," Zargathesey said solemnly.

"Good to know," Wade whispered. He had the suspicion that if he spoke in his normal voice he would set the wounds to paining something awful again.

"Of course," Zargathesey said in mock modesty, "you'd of been dead, it wasn't for my skills and handi-work."

Amanda was shocked once again, and she stared at the medical man like he had lost his mind.

Calhoun shrugged tentatively. It was an uncomfortable movement, but not agonizing. "I suppose," he said. He did not find the doctor humorous in the least.

At least he thought the physician was trying to be humorous.

"Think you can eat some?" Zargathesey asked, unfazed by Calhoun's lack of enthusiasm.

"I reckon."

"You need it. You've been out the better part of two weeks. And you've lost a heap of blood, son. You'll need to rebuild your blood and so your strength. Food'll do wonders for you." He looked at Amanda. "You'll see he gets something?"

"Yes, sir," Amanda said enthusiastically.

"Nothing more than broth, mind you."

"Yessir."

"You get well soon, boy," Zargathesey said, glaring at Calhoun.

"Your concern is touchin'," Calhoun said dryly.

"It ain't concern for your health so much, son. I just need the bed for folks who're really ailing."

Calhoun craned his neck around cautiously. It increased the pain some but not enough to stop him. He was the only one in a bed in the room. "Oh?" he asked, sarcasm creeping into his low voice.

Zargathesey moved his head, as if that would help him evade the question. "Well, that and the fact that if you don't mend soon, it'll reflect poorly on my doctoring skills."

"Can't have that," Calhoun whispered in flat tones.

"Sure can't." Zargathesey snapped his bag shut and marched out the door without another word. Amanda followed, tentatively, after telling Calhoun she would return directly.

Calhoun lay there, thinking about Doctor Zargathesey. It helped him keep his mind off the pain of his wounds. He was not sure what he thought about the physician. Zargathesey was competent enough, that was obvious. But there was something about the man that grated on Calhoun.

Amanda was not gone long. Her simple presence pushed Zargathesey—and even some of the tremendous pain—out of Calhoun's consciousness.

Amanda sat close to the bed and spoon-fed Calhoun some elk broth. Calhoun slurped up the soup greedily. He wished there was something in it that he could sink his teeth into. But there wasn't, and he knew he would be wasting his breath by asking for it. He tried to be satisfied with what he had.

After eating his fill, he lay back and closed his eyes. The last thing he remembered before sleep overtook him was the cool softness of Amanda's hand on his forehead.

CHAPTER
* 18 *

It was more than another month before Calhoun could venture outside— other than for short, quick trips to the outhouse. By then, winter had wrapped the land in a cold, white blanket.

Calhoun had spent the entire time in Doctor Zargathesey's small hospital, though he chafed at it. As soon as he had awoken the first time, he wanted to be up and about as quickly as possible.

He knew in his head that he was incapable of anything at the time, including the most rudimentary needs of nature. But his heart wanted him active and mobile, as if that would wash away the pain and the wounds.

He managed to restrain himself. He was aided by the blunt, dry humor of Doctor Janeck Zargathesey, and the stern orders of Miss Amanda Powell.

He did convince his two wardens, as he considered Amanda and Zargathesey, to allow him to begin moving a little in the room a week after he woke. He made it a point after that to get up at least three times daily and shuffle a few steps more each day.

By the end of that week, he could manage his personal needs himself. To him, that was a major breakthrough. He was considerably embarrassed to have to ask Zargathesey—or worse, Amanda—to help him in such matters.

His first trip to the outhouse out back of Zargathesey's was something of an adventure. But he made it there and back in one piece. It was the first time he had been out of doors in more than a month.

About that time, Sheriff McCloskey appeared and asked him to tell what had happened.

Calhoun was a man of few words, so he gave the lawman a verbal sketch of what had happened.

McCloskey sat, nodding, occasionally scribbling a note on some dirty paper with a pen dipped in a small crystal inkwell. When Calhoun had finished—in a surprisingly short time, McCloskey thought—the sheriff asked, "The others still roamin' around?"

"I expect," Calhoun answered sourly. He did not like leaving business unfinished. Especially business like this. Such things had a tendency to come back and haunt people.

"You know where they are?"

"No more'n last time."

"What're you gonna do about. . . ?"

"That's enough questions now, Sheriff," Amanda said sharply. She figured that if she didn't step in, the two men might come to blows. Calhoun was in no shape for such activity. She knew that Calhoun would go after Garth Nichols and the rest of the outlaws as soon as he was able. The sheriff should've known that too, she figured.

McCloskey left unsatisfied. He attempted to elicit some information on Calhoun's plans several more times. But he was thwarted at every turn by a diligent

Amanda Powell. So the lawman finally gave it up.

It was almost another month after Calhoun's first trip to the outhouse before he made a real trip outside. And that was to go "home," to his room at Mother Powell's boarding house.

That was a great day for him. Amanda brought over some of the new clothes he had gotten at Adolph Blenheim's store so long ago and never had a chance to wear. Since Mister Spranger had been killed, there was no barber in town, so Amanda volunteered to shave Calhoun. With trepidation, he agreed.

The results were better than Calhoun had expected. He suffered far fewer nicks and cuts than he did when he shaved himself or had a barber do it. He realized that Amanda had a deft, steady hand and a smooth gentle touch. Though the touch was innocent, it gave him thoughts that were not as pure as they might have been.

After the shave, he managed a quick bath. Despite the buckets of hot water poured into the tub, the frigid temperatures outside soon chilled the room—and the water. Calhoun shivered a little as he ran a scratchy towel over his flesh. Then he quickly dressed.

He ran a comb through his hair. First time in years for this, he thought wryly. He pulled on the heavy, flannel-lined canvas coat. Settling the already worn hat on his still-damp hair, he stepped into the examining room.

Only Zargathesey and Amanda were there, which was a great relief to him. Amanda said nothing but Zargathesey could not resist.

"Hell, had I known this was going to be a coming out

party, I would've dressed for the occasion," he noted dryly. He was wearing his customary off-white cotton shirt, string tie, black lace-up boots, black wool trousers, and matching frock coat. No one could ever recall seeing him wearing anything else.

Calhoun just glared at the physician.

"Come on," Amanda said. In the past month and a half, she had become increasingly exasperated with the physician, and his feeble attempts at humor.

Amanda slipped her right hand between Calhoun's left arm and his body. She looked up at him, making sure it was all right.

Calhoun had a momentary flash of anger. *How dare she try to treat me like I was helpless!* he thought in a rage.

Then he realized he might need help. The woman's action had been natural. No one would notice that she was helping him. It would simply look like she was walking arm in arm with him. He nodded once, almost imperceptibly.

"Thanks, Doc," Calhoun said as he and Amanda headed for the door.

Zargathesey shrugged. He had been paid by Amanda. That was all that mattered to him. Or so he tried to tell himself.

Actually, he rather liked Calhoun. And he had attempted, with humor, to draw the younger man out of his shell of hatred and anger. He knew he had not been successful in the least, and that bothered the old physician.

Zargathesey thought that perhaps he was getting too old for this business. He considered retiring and giving his practice over to Pavel. But then he realized that he would die without his work.

Calhoun and Amanda stepped out into the cold night. A frigid wind was blowing, snapping the ends of his coat and her shawl. A hint of snow was in the air.

But Calhoun had insisted on leaving the doctor's infirmary at night. That way there would be no prying eyes, no pointed fingers, no gawking citizens.

Amanda adjusted her pace to Calhoun's slow shuffle. Calhoun appreciated the gesture but said nothing. He just moved along, trying to stand as erect as possible. Most of the real pain was gone, though he still suffered little lancing jabs of it every now and again. It was nothing he could not handle.

What bothered him the most was the weakness. He felt like a child again. He had always been thin, but now he had lost weight. And with the loss of weight and blood came depleted strength. Calhoun had always been proud of the power contained in his lithe, rope-like muscles. But now he felt like he would collapse without Amanda's support. That sickened him.

Calhoun was greatly relieved to enter his room at the boarding house. He had a small twinge of disgust at the starkness of the room—which reflected the starkness of his life. But he put it down to his depleted condition.

Amanda helped him, until he was sitting on the bed. She pushed gently on his good shoulder, wanting him to lie down. But he resisted.

"You've done well, Mister Calhoun," she said quietly. Her voice firmed. "But you still need a little help. And plenty of rest. Now lay down." She shoved lightly again.

Calhoun could see no more reason to resist it. The short walk—combined with the cold weather—had sapped his already meager strength. He was exhausted. He let himself be shoved down.

He was still awake as Amanda lifted his legs onto the bed. He never did feel her pulling off his boots or covering him up. He was asleep already.

Calhoun gained strength and confidence with each passing day. His appetite was voracious, and at times he thought he might eat Amanda's restaurant out of business. Amanda did not seem to mind feeding him five or six times a day, and always fed him huge amounts of victuals.

Indeed, Amanda seemed to think quite highly of Calhoun. The two were often seen walking together through the cold, snowy streets of Cimarron. A number of people were even heard to comment that they made a nice couple.

Calhoun ignored the talk. He didn't quite ignore Amanda, but he did not encourage her attentions either. He would not—could not—fall in love. He had work to be done yet. And there was always the memory of Lizbeth.

Still, he liked her attentions, and could see no reason not to have a fling with her, if the opportunity arose. He would not force himself on any woman in that way. And since she was a respectable woman, he thought the chances of a dalliance with Amanda Powell were quite remote.

Amanda, for her part, had concluded that life with Calhoun would not be all pleasant. He was a handsome enough man, in a rugged sort of way. And he was certainly polite enough. He was strong, considerate and all man. But he was not as giving as she might hope. And she knew he would never be able to give of himself fully.

None of that meant she couldn't enjoy his presence, though. Or encourage some attention from him.

She came to realize over the next several weeks that she would have to be blunt and direct if she expected any more attention from him than he might give a sister. Such a move on her part was risky, she knew, but she had inherited her mother's fearlessness and disregard for the conventional.

After several weeks, Calhoun was nearly back to normal. He was still weak, but he was getting around well. He had been out behind the boarding house every day, practicing with his pistols. To an outsider, it would seem that he had never lost his "shooting eye." But he knew he had lost some of his proficiency because of his prolonged recovery.

He could feel his strength coming back, though he knew it would be a few more months at least before he was fully recovered. He was still eating well, and he slept peacefully.

Life was good, except for the fact that he wanted to be out after the last of the outlaws who had killed Mother Powell. That thought—and urgency—was never far from his mind. He willed himself to stay patient. He knew that to go out in his condition, especially in winter, would be dangerous. Possibly fatal. He must wait.

Each night, as he lay in his bed, he would stretch and tense, testing his muscles. The pain was there at first, but lessened over time until it was but a lingering bad memory. He was beginning to feel more like himself.

He was going through his ritual one night, just before Christmas, when Amanda knocked on the door and called for entrance.

"Wait," he shouted. Calhoun pulled the covers up to his neck. Though he was wearing his longjohns, he did not want Amanda to see him like that. He didn't think it was proper. "Come in," he called, when he was covered.

Amanda entered tentatively at first. But she had made up her mind. With the remembrance of her resolve, her doubts fled. She marched up to the bed.

"Evenin', Mister Calhoun," she said evenly.

Calhoun looked up at her. Amanda's hair was loose. It flowed in cascades down onto her shoulders. Her face was scrubbed clean. She wore only a nightdress of white cotton. It was loose and billowy, and covered little of her roundness, especially with the low light glowing from the lantern on the table behind her. Calhoun wondered what Amanda was up to.

"Evenin', ma'am," he ventured.

They both waited, as silence stretched on.

"It's cold out here . . . Wade," Amanda said.

He nodded, not sure what to say.

Amanda decided she would have to be even more direct. She had resolved that this was what she wanted to do, and she was bound to see it through. She reached up and untied the knot at her throat. The night dress sifted down to her bare feet like a soft cloud.

"Good Lord," Calhoun breathed. But he was no fool. He shoved over on the bed and turned down the covers on the side where Amanda stood. She clambered in, shivering. "Goose bumps ain't becomin'," she said, teeth chattering a little.

Calhoun made no comment. He simply turned toward her, lips searching for hers. She responded willingly.

"This don't change anything between us, you know," Calhoun said later.

"I know." Amanda had no regrets about any of this.

"Then why?" Calhoun asked. He was surprised. He had thought she would expect this to make him love her or something. And he didn't want to have to hurt her to let her know that it would not work.

Amanda shrugged. She was snuggled up against him. The wind howled outside, tearing at the wood sides of the rooming house. "Kind of hard to explain," she finally said. "Ma never did go in much for convention. I expect she passed that along to me." Amanda flushed a little, embarrassed, but she thought Calhoun had a right to hear about it. "It wasn't unusual for Ma to have a man when the notion struck her."

"Nothin' wrong in that," Calhoun said honestly. He wasn't planning on marrying Amanda. If they both saw this for what it was, then it could be enjoyable. He reached for her again.

CHAPTER

✳ 19 ✳

Amanda screeched in surprise when she hit the floor hard and bounced on her bare bottom. She wondered what had broken the glass. But no matter what it was, she didn't think it a good reason for Calhoun to dump her out of bed.

She scowled, ready to poke her head up over the edge of the bed. Her mouth was already forming the words with which she planned to scold Calhoun.

But she shut up fast and dropped flat on the floor at the report of gunshots.

The gunfire was loud in the small room, but Amanda could still hear several bullets hit the bed.

Then she heard the heavy cough of one of Calhoun's Colt Dragoons. There was a short, sharp gasp of pain outside. Then the sound of running. Finally, silence.

"You all right, Amanda?" Calhoun asked. He sat in the bed, covers bunched around his waist. He still held the smoking Colt in his hand, and he was watching the window.

"Yes." Amanda was surprised to learn she still had a voice, considering how frightened she was.

"Best get up and dress. Quickly," he ordered.

As she hurriedly threw on her nightdress, she realized the wisdom of it. While she might defy convention when it suited her purposes, she knew it was not wise to flaunt such defiance in public too often.

She had been here every night but one for the past week, and no one was the wiser for it. But if she was caught here, naked, it would go badly for her in the eyes of the townsfolk.

Amanda knew she was not the only "decent" woman who did things like she had last night. Far from it. But the trick to it all was secrecy. Like those many others, she knew enough to at least present a conventional face to the world.

With her shift on, Amanda flew to the door. She yanked it open, stepped out, turned and yelled for help.

Melba and several residents of the boarding home opened their doors cautiously. They had, of course, heard the gunshots. But they did not want to get involved with any gunplay.

Still, when they saw Amanda standing there in her nightdress, her hair loose and feet uncovered, they figured it was safe enough to come out. They even felt a grudging respect for the beautiful young woman, who had boldly rushed out of her own room and toward the sound of the gunfire. And to do it when she didn't even know what to expect! Well, that was certainly something.

The people began edging out of their rooms and toward Calhoun's room.

"Someone—Mister Allen—please go fetch the sheriff," Amanda commanded, cool and graceful.

A tall, mostly bald, bespectacled man bobbed his

bony head and skittered off, the tails of his robe flying behind him. The tinware drummer made a comical sight in his nightshirt, robe and untied boots.

"If you'd close the door, ma'am," Calhoun suggested softly, politely.

Amanda nodded. She shut the door, feeling a flush of pride that she—with Calhoun's help—had managed to fool all the others. She could see in their faces that they had no suspicions of her recent activity.

McCloskey arrived a few minutes later. He looked rumpled, having just been woken. Dawn was still some hours off. It was just before midnight, he saw by the clock in the hallway and he was not kindly disposed toward having been disturbed.

Amanda rapped on the door. "Mister Calhoun," she called lightly. "Sheriff McCloskey is here."

"Open up!" McCloskey bellowed.

"Stop your yellin'," Calhoun said as he pulled the door open. He glared at the lawman.

McCloskey ignored him. He shoved into the room and asked, "What's goin' on here?"

Calhoun explained in two or three clipped sentences. He was in no mood to listen to McCloskey's bluster.

"Harumph," McCloskey growled. "Let's go on outside and see what we can find."

"Good idea," Calhoun offered dryly.

McCloskey shot daggers from his eyes at Calhoun. He shoved his way through the door and encountered the boardinghouse residents. "Go on back in your rooms!" he roared angrily. "All of you. There ain't nothin' for you here."

McCloskey and Calhoun walked out into the freezing night and around the corner of the building. The body was not hard to find. It was lying on the ground under Calhoun's window. Its left eye was gone, replaced by a bloody bullet hole. Another bullet hole dotted its forehead.

"Know him?" McCloskey asked. He was still tired and irritable. But at least he had not been roused for nothing. Still, this would mean extra work for him.

"Nope."

"Dammit, Wade," McCloskey snapped. "If . . . " he got a grip on his exploding temper and wrestled it under control. "You sure?" he asked more calmly.

"Yep."

"Then why the hell was he tryin' to kill you?" McCloskey squinted at the saddle tramp in the darkness broken only by the pale illumination from the oil street lamp.

Calhoun shrugged. He had been wondering just that since the gunsmoke had cleared, and he was no closer to an answer now than he was then. However, he had every intention of finding out, and of discouraging any further such efforts.

"Shit," McCloskey said. His annoyance grew. But now it was the annoyance of facing what likely would be an impossible task, not the annoyance of being woken in the middle of the night.

He scuffed the toe of his boot in the snow. "You said there was another one?" he asked.

"I heard one runnin'.."

McCloskey looked up at the thick, dark clouds. Snow sifted down lightly. "Ain't snowin' too hard," he commented, dropping his gaze to meet Calhoun's eyes. "Might be able to trail him."

Calhoun had wondered how long it would take the sheriff to come to such an obvious conclusion. But all he said was, "Might."

McCloskey shot a sharp glance at Calhoun before moving off.

Calhoun quickly moved into the lead. He found the footprints in a minute. Usually Calhoun did not like snow very much, but he appreciated this gentle snow-fall. Any old snow would be mushy; it would yield no tracks. A heavier snowfall would cover up any tracks too quickly.

This light drifting left enough on the ground to keep imprints without burying them almost immediately.

Calhoun followed the footprints all the way to the back door of Becker's Billiards Parlor.

"You want to go on in and get him, Wade?" McCloskey asked. He was feeling a little mellower now, though he wasn't sure why. He assumed it was because he figured that this nonsense was about to come to an end.

"Yep," Calhoun said, anger tightening his face. He paused. "But I'll wait," he added.

"Huh?" McCloskey asked surprised. He stopped with his hand on the latch, ready to open the door. He looked back over his shoulder.

"I got no idea what he looks like. Never saw him." As much as he'd like to blast the bastard that almost killed him and Amanda, he could not just go in and recklessly start shooting at anyone he saw.

"Snow on his shoes?" McCloskey suggested helpfully.

He dropped his hand and turned.

"Could be somebody else just come in."

McCloskey grimaced, knowing it was futile. "What do you suggest, then?" he asked.

"I'll think of something."

McCloskey looked sharply at Calhoun again. He was on the verge of asking what Calhoun was brewing up. But he decided against it. He didn't want to know. If he found out, he might be duty-bound to try to stop it. That very well could be a lot more difficult than he wanted to face.

He simply nodded and said, "Just try not to make it too messy." He shuddered involuntarily as he walked away.

Calhoun waited a few minutes, standing there in the cold. He was formulating a plan and wanted to let it gel without interference. Finally it was as set as it was going to be.

It wasn't much of a plan, he admitted mentally as he walked down the snowy street. But it was all he could think of. He figured that whoever it was who had tried to kill him must have some connection with Willy Becker. The billiards parlor owner was not the type of man to leave the back door of his business open. Therefore, the man who had tried to kill Calhoun and Amanda either had a key to the place, or he knew it would be open.

Calhoun figured another talk with Becker was needed.

Calhoun hurried through the snow back to the boardinghouse. Amanda was waiting outside his room for him. She followed him inside. Calhoun took off his coat and began dressing more warmly. He even shoved a pair of leather gloves into his coat pocket and tossed the garment back on the bed.

"Where're you going?" Amanda asked as he worked.

"Got business to tend to."

"At this hour?"

"Yep."

"Where? What. . . ?" Calhoun's look shut her up and frightened her.

"It's none of your concern," Calhoun said curtly. He pulled his coat back on.

"Don't expect me to be waitin' for you when you come back," Amanda said petulantly. She was hurt by Calhoun's behavior and she wanted him to know it. Despite that hurt, she never doubted that he would be back. She just could not see him getting killed by anyone.

Calhoun shrugged. "I understand," he said. He walked out the door, closing it tightly behind him. Right now he didn't much care if he ever saw her again. There was more important business to tend to than assuaging Amanda Powell's hurt feelings. If she couldn't see that, she would find no relief in his explanation.

He hustled through the mostly quiet streets of Cimarron. The snow had increased marginally, and the wind whipped the soft snowfall into an icy curtain that tore at his face.

Calhoun took up the same post at the corner of Becker's Billiards Parlor that he had taken several months earlier. He pulled on his gloves and waited.

Becker was one of the first out this night. He pulled

the collar of his coat up around his ears and hurried off. As he walked swiftly past the corner of the building, Calhoun reached out and grabbed him by the shoulder.

Before Becker could make a sound, Calhoun had spun him around and slammed his face into the side of the building. Becker groaned and sagged. Calhoun held him up.

"You call for help and I'll batter your face into the wall again," Calhoun snarled.

"What do you want?" Becker asked. He felt a fear inside that was colder than the night's temperature.

"Some of your time."

"What're we gonna do?"

"Wait."

"For what?"

"Shut up, Willy."

Becker quickly closed his mouth. He needed to urinate very badly, and he clamped his legs closed against the fright-spawned feeling. Almost absently, he reached up and touched his left ear. His fear intensified considerably.

CHAPTER

* 20 *

Calhoun shoved Becker into a chair, which almost toppled over backward from the force. "What the hell do you want?" Becker asked, his face an ivory mask of fear. His voice bobbled and shook.

"To chat," Calhoun growled. He took off his gloves and coat and dropped them on a billiards table at his right side.

Calhoun picked up a pool cue from the same table and hefted it by the slim end in his right hand, testing its weight and suppleness. In his left hand, he held a dirty rag used to clean the bar that he had scooped up as he entered the room.

"I've got nothin' to say to you, Calhoun," Becker said defiantly, trying to cover up his fear with bluster. He rested his right arm on the billiards table next to him. He hoped he might distract Calhoun a moment and grab one of the hard billiard balls on the table and toss it at Calhoun. Then he could run like hell. He realized it wasn't much of a plan, but it was all he could think of in his fearful state.

"For a man with nothin' to say, Willy, you sure do talk a heap," Calhoun commented calmly.

Suddenly, Calhoun whipped the pool cue forward. The butt end cracked on Becker's right forearm. The bone snapped.

It took an instant for the realization of the pain to hit Becker. His eyes widened as he looked at Calhoun in horror. As he opened his mouth to scream, Calhoun jammed the filthy, odorous bar rag into the billiards parlor owner's mouth.

When he saw the scream gone from Becker's face, Calhoun pulled the rag out of the man's mouth. "Who came to kill me tonight?" he asked, voice hard and cold.

The usually dapper little man was sweating. Pain raced through his arm, and he was afraid to move it. He tried to spit out the foul taste left behind by the filthy cloth. The nauseating taste of the rag, drenched in whiskey, beer and tobacco, made him gag.

"I don't know what you're talking . . ."

Calhoun was out of patience. He jammed the soiled rag back into Becker's mouth and then set about beating the billiards parlor owner with controlled rage.

Becker jerked and shook, trying to avoid the rain of blows from the flying pool cue. But he was confined to the chair by Calhoun's raging fury, and there was no escape for him.

Calhoun was methodical. He tempered his anger with ruthless efficiency. The pool cue flew through the air, landing with solid thuds. Ribs cracked, a femur broke and finger bones snapped.

Calhoun's savage assault left only one part of Becker's body untouched — his head. Calhoun did not want an unconscious man on his hands. All he wanted was a softened, compliant billiards parlor owner, a man who was willing to talk and speak the truth.

After ten minutes, Calhoun stopped. He stood back a moment, breathing hard. Still somewhat weak from the bullet wounds, his breathing came a little hard. But he was pleased with himself. His body had reacted well. A few more weeks at most and he would be back to his old self completely, he figured.

He set the pool cue down on the billiards table with deliberate gentleness. Then he rolled a cigarette and stuck the tube in his mouth. Pulling a match from a shirt pocket, he scraped it across his belt and held the small flame to the cigarette. He flicked the still-burning match at Becker.

The match hit Becker's chest and fell into his lap. Becker lurched backward, knocking the chair over. He landed on his right side, wincing as his broken arm hit the floor. The match fell by the wayside and died out.

Becker lay on the floor, whimpering. His nose was clogged with mucus from crying. That, and the foul rag still jammed in his mouth, made breathing almost impossible. For a moment, Becker thought he would suffocate.

Calhoun crouched in front of Becker and tugged the rag free. He tossed it aside. Becker choked and spit and sucked in great gobs of air, but his eyes were dulled with pain.

"I told you once before, Willy, that I'm a man of little patience," Calhoun said quietly. There was an iron menace underlying the soft words. "I'll ask you this only one more time. Who came to kill me tonight?"

Becker wheezed and whimpered. Small moans bubbled up and out, unbidden. Calhoun let him recover a few moments.

"Two men," Becker finally gasped. "Jeremy Brancus and Rance Quade." He spit, gagging on the remains of the disgusting rag. Tremors shook him as pains lanced into him at one spot and then another, moving about his body like a peripatetic plague of locusts.

"Only Quade come back," Becker added, almost as an afterthought.

Calhoun nodded. "Who sent 'em?" He suspected Becker, but he could not be sure.

"Me." The dapper little man's bitterness overrode his fear for several moments.

"Why?" Calhoun was sure he knew that, too, but he wanted to hear it from Becker.

"Why the hell do you think?" Becker snarled, voice bloated by pain. He lifted his mangled left hand and gingerly touched his ear. The appendage was attached, but old Doctor Zargathesey had done a rather poor job of it. The ragged line where it had been sewn on was obvious, and the seam was discolored with dirt. The scar seemed red and inflamed.

Calhoun nodded. It answered several questions for him. But it did nothing to assuage his anger. He was angry at Becker for having sent men to kill him, and for not having the courage to face him himself.

Calhoun was also angry at himself. He should have killed Becker the last time. Even if the billiards parlor owner had lied to him—which seemed a possibility now—he would have saved himself a considerable amount of grief by having dispatched Becker earlier.

That was all gone by now, and he could not change the past. He could, however, make sure he did not make the mistake a second time. But that would have to wait just a little longer. He needed more answers.

Calhoun pushed up. Jamming the smoldering cigarette between his lips, he bent and righted the chair. He dropped the cigarette on the floor and stamped it out with the toe of his boot. Then he lifted Becker into the chair.

Becker's system had gone into shock, and the pain was far less than he might have imagined. Still, the jostling of all the broken bones left him weeping. He settled into the chair, and the searing pain began to return with a vengeance. He could find no comfortable way to sit, no way in which cracked bones were not rubbing against each other.

"Where's this Quade now?" Calhoun asked quietly.

Becker thought of lying. Then the pain that inundated his system made him realize the foolishness of such a thought. He knew there was only one way to save himself—tell this madman the truth.

"Ain't sure exactly," Becker said. He gasped in fear as he saw the flicker of suddenly renewed rage on Calhoun's face. "Wait, please," he said, not caring that he was whining.

"He's got a room over at the Cimarron Queen Hotel," Becker added hastily. "He was here a while, then left. I ain't sure if he went back to his room."

"He ain't left town?"

"I don't think so," Becker allowed. He tried to smile, but his agony wouldn't allow it. "He told me you took out Brancus. He was tempted to stay to rub you out himself, just on principle. I encouraged that by upping the price I was going to pay."

Becker shrugged, as if unconcerned. Shooting pains

through his torso left him gasping in misery.

"He aimin' to get help to come after me?" Calhoun was unfazed by the information.

"Don't know. He ain't done so yet though." Becker's words were garbled a little, as he tried to talk through the pain.

Calhoun believed him. Quade would not have had enough time to hire another gunmen—yet. It was another loose end Calhoun would have to take care of. And soon.

"What room's he in?"

"Don't know. Honest."

"What's he look like?"

"You don't know?" Becker responded, surprised.

Calhoun stared evenly at Becker. If Becker knew he had not seen this Quade, Becker very well might lie about the man's appearance, he figured. But if Becker was unsure if Calhoun knew much about him, the billiards parlor owner should be scared enough to tell the truth.

Becker had the same thoughts. He knew it was wiser to tell the truth here. The chance that Calhoun knew something about Quade was too great a risk for him to lie.

"A man about your height. A little stockier," Becker said, and began to warm to the task. Rance Quade came with a big reputation as a man who could handle himself. Becker suddenly decided that the quicker he could get Calhoun to face Quade, the faster Quade would dispatch Calhoun.

"Has a scar over his right eye. A mashed nose. His two front teeth are missin'."

Calhoun nodded. Quade should be easy enough to find. He had heard the name before, and knew a little of the man's reputation. He did not think he would have any trouble in taking the gunman.

"Where's Garth?" Calhoun asked quietly after a few minutes' pause.

A gust of wintry wind puffed up outside and rattled the building a moment before drifting on.

"Wasn't he in Cimarron Canyon?" Becker asked blandly.

"If he was there when I went lookin' for him, he'd be buried there," Calhoun said evenly. "Now, where the hell is he?"

"Don't know." Becker was afraid to try to shrug again.

Calhoun punched Becker in the front of one side. Several already broken ribs caved in.

Becker's eyes rolled up in his head, and his consciousness began to fade. Calhoun pinched the man's right earlobe between two fingers. "Don't you faint, boy," he snarled.

The sharp, short pain snapped Becker back to consciousness. He groaned.

"Where's Nichols?" Calhoun asked again.

Becker knew the question would not be repeated. He no longer had enough strength to lie. "Black Water. That's where he was plannin' to spend the winter." Becker drew in a careful breath. It still hurt like all hellfire. "He might go out now and again lookin' for some easy pickin's."

Calhoun nodded. "You get him warnin' when I went lookin' for him last time?"

"Yes," Becker nodded. He was defeated. "Told him to keep away from Cimarron Canyon for a spell and to lay low." He wanted to die, he thought, since in death there would be no more pain.

Calhoun nodded again. He had suspected as much. "He plannin' to come back here?"

"He ain't said." Becker looked at Calhoun with pain-bleared eyes. "I suspect, though, that he will."

Calhoun smiled viciously. He would expect Nichols to do so. A man like Nichols would not let someone like Calhoun get away with killing most of the members of his gang without exacting retribution. Calhoun would do the same in Nichols's position.

"Anything else you'd like to tell me?" Calhoun asked in a flat voice.

Becker licked his lips. He was certain Calhoun would kill him as soon as he stopped talking. But his brain, clouded by the agony of his wounds, was not functioning well. He could think of nothing else to say. Well, he could think of a few things, but the insults would only antagonize this crazy saddle tramp even further.

"No," he whispered. While he knew that death would end his pain, Becker realized he really didn't want to die. Still, he was resigned to it.

"Obliged," Calhoun said, not meaning it. He pulled on his coat and picked up his gloves. He turned and started walking toward the door, pulling on his left glove.

Becker looked up in surprise. Despite the agony that infested him from head to foot, hope blossomed in his heart. The fool was going to let him live! He would get over these injuries. And if, by some chance, Calhoun killed Quade, Becker would hire an even better gunman, the best that money could buy, to take care of this arrogant son of a bitch.

Becker watched Calhoun walk away. He was too filled with pain to move just yet, but elation began to fill him with strength. He figured that as soon as Calhoun was out the door, he would be able to get up and walk—or crawl—for help.

Calhoun stopped at the door. He turned, and Becker realized with horror that Calhoun had one of his big pistols in hand. A cruel smile curled across Calhoun's lips.

"You didn't really think I'd let you live after what you tried to do to me, did you?" he said in quiet menace.

The pistol bucked once in Calhoun's hand. He shoved the pistol into the holster, and stepped outside. He stopped and pulled on his other glove. Then he walked unhurriedly down the street, in the direction of the Cimarron Queen Hotel.

CHAPTER

✳ 21 ✳

The Cimarron Queen Hotel was a shabby building on the bank of the rushing Cimarron River. Several plank boards rattled in the wintry wind and the three stairs groaned under his weight as Calhoun walked inside.

An old man slept behind the counter. He sat on a stool, his back and head resting against the corner. Calhoun stepped behind the counter and shook the old man's arm roughly.

The man's lids lifted, exposing bleary eyes. The gray-haired head shifted, and he looked bleakly at Calhoun. He worked his tongue in and out a few times, trying to work up spit. The movement made his false teeth clatter in his mouth.

"Whaddaya want?" he asked. He was irritated at having been so rudely awakened, but he was also afraid of the hard-eyed man who glared at him.

"What room's Rance Quade in?" Calhoun asked harshly.

"I don't know," the man said. His annoyance grew once he decided that he was too old to be afraid.

"Look," Calhoun ordered.

The old man's thinking shifted again. While he still thought he might be too old to be frightened, he realized he really didn't want to die for nothing. He hopped off the stool, quite sprightly despite his sixty-seven years. He thumbed through the pages of an old ledger on the counter.

Calhoun waited, trying to be patient. The wind whistled through spaces between the boards, chilling the building. He was glad he was wearing his coat.

"Number Eleven," the old man said. He pointed down a hallway to his left. "Third door on the right." He rubbed his hands quickly up and down his arms, trying to warm them by reviving the circulation.

"Got a key?" Calhoun asked.

The man rummaged around on the desk and in the bins behind the counter. Finally he came up with a key. He handed it to Calhoun. He said nothing.

"Obliged," Calhoun said distractedly. He turned and walked down the hall.

The old man watched for a moment. He rubbed his arms again and shivered. "Damn winter," he grumbled. He reached under the counter and retrieved a thin blanket. Throwing it around his shoulders, he climbed back onto his stool. He pulled the blanket tight around him and rested his head into the angle of the two walls. With a sigh of contentment, he drifted back to sleep.

Calhoun walked silently down the dingy, shabby hallway. He stopped at the third door. It was unmarked by a number. He shrugged and quietly inserted the key into the lock. Leaving it there, Calhoun pulled off his gloves. With his right hand he brought out one of the Dragoons. With his left, he turned the key.

The door creaked open wide with a slight shove from Calhoun, but he remained outside, just to the right of the opening. He waited, listening intently. All he could hear was the shrill droning of the wind as it found entrance to the building through the many cracks and spaces.

There was no reaction from inside. Calhoun cursed himself silently. He should have just burst into the room. That most likely would have been enough to startle anyone inside. That—and his movement—should have flustered them enough to miss their first shot. Calhoun could have then used the muzzle flash as a target and finished this little bit of business quickly.

It was too late for that now. He took off his hat and hung it over the barrel of his pistol and edged the crown of the hat out past the doorjamb.

Nothing happened.

Calhoun pulled his hat back and put it on again. Either Quade was made of steel and not fooled by the ploy, or he was not inside.

Calhoun believed the latter. The hallway was illuminated only by a single oil lantern. The stinking, smoky lamp provided enough light that anyone inside would have seen the hat, but not so much as to make it apparent that there wasn't a person wearing it. Calhoun figured Quade would not have been able to resist firing.

Calhoun kept the Dragoon in hand as he slid his back along the doorjamb and entered the room. He flattened his back against the inside wall. The revolver was raised, cocked and ready. His eyes surveyed the room.

It was dark in the room, but the lantern in the hall-way threw enough light that Calhoun could see it was empty. He relaxed and uncocked his revolver. After putting it away, he retrieved the key, shut the door and locked it.

He stumbled across the pitch dark room to the lantern on the table. He lighted it, keeping the flame low. Then he looked around. In a pair of saddlebags hanging over the bedpost, he found a bottle of whiskey. He took it.

Calhoun uncorked the bottle, put it on the table and sat. Turning the lamp down so that it was almost out, he rolled a cigarette. He sat sipping the poor, cheap whiskey and smoking.

He judged that almost an hour had passed before he heard a scrabbling sound at the door. He quickly stabbed out his cigarette and pulled a Dragoon, thumbed back the hammer, and waited.

The door swung open and slammed against the wall behind it. A burly man entered, mumbling drunkenly. A woman followed him in, and then another man. As the first man's face flashed briefly in the hallway light, Calhoun could see a scar above the right eye and a wide, flattened nose.

Calhoun discounted the woman. She was a prosti-tute, and a cheap one at that. He figured she neither cared about these men, nor would she cause trouble when something happened to them.

The second man was something of a problem for Calhoun. He figured the man either was a partner of Quade's, or had just been hired by Quade to help take Calhoun. It didn't matter either way.

"It don't pay to leave a job unfinished, Quade," Calhoun said quietly.

"Wha . . .?" Quade mumbled. He looked around the dark room, weaving drunkenly.

Calhoun turned the small key on the lantern, flooding the room with flickering yellow light. "Runnin' when you've botched a job ain't too smart, Quade."

"Calhoun!" Quade breathed.

"Yep." Calhoun fired twice.

Quade jerked once and then again as the lead balls punctured his chest and heart. He banged against the wall then fell forward. He hit the floor after bouncing off the bed. Except for muscles that twitched involuntarily, Quade did not move.

Calhoun did not bother to watch Quade fall. He knew from experience that Quade was a goner.

He swung the cocked Dragoon around toward the other man who threw his hands into the air.

"Whoa, mister," he said, an edge of nervousness in his voice.

Calhoun glanced at the woman. "You belong to either of these fellers?"

"No." Her voice was a whisper. She had seen men killed before. But none so swiftly and with such callous disregard. "Just . . ." She found it odd that she was embarrassed to mention that the two men had just bought her favors.

Calhoun nodded. "Then get."

The woman needed no encouragement. She fled. The memory of those hard eyes, and the ruthlessness of Quade's death would linger with her for a long time.

It would also, she vowed, keep her from reporting this to anyone.

"You got a name, boy?" Calhoun asked the other man harshly.

"Billy." He clamped his mouth shut.

Calhoun nodded. He needed no second name. Many men would give only one name under the best of circumstances.

Billy was in his mid-twenties, a little younger than Calhoun. He was tall and stout, with a boyish face, long hair and clear eyes. Light fuzz covered the lower half of his face.

"What's your connection to Quade?" Calhoun asked.

"Just met him." Billy winced inwardly. He knew that sounded bad, especially considering who Calhoun was.

"We was in the saloon together," he added lamely. "Neither of us had a whole lot of cash." He looked rueful. "I lost all I had but two bucks in a card game."

"So?"

Calhoun's tone chilled Billy. "Mind if I put my arms down?" he asked innocently. He wanted any sort of advantage he could get. With his arms down, he might be able to get to a pistol if Calhoun somehow got distracted. He wasn't sure it would do him any good. It seemed likely that he was going to die. And if that was true, he would want to go down making some kind of effort. Not standing here with his hands in the air.

Calhoun shrugged. The young man did not worry him.

Billy dropped his arms slowly. Blood rushed back

into them, making them tingle a little. Moving cautiously, he lightly hooked his thumbs into his gunbelt.

Calhoun had made no move, and Billy figured that so far, so good. Maybe this Calhoun wasn't as good as people thought he was.

"So?" Calhoun said again.

"Oh," Billy said with a weak smile, "yeah. Well, anyways, me and Quade there got to be talkin'. We decided we wanted us a woman." He smiled bashfully. "But seein's how neither of us had much money . . ." He shrugged.

After a breath, he said, "We put our money together and come up with enough for . . . for . . . well . . . anyways, we talked Brown Eyes there into takin' us both on for the price of one. Cash up front."

"That the only business proposition you two entered in?" Calhoun asked, eyes burning at Billy.

"Yep." Billy seemed at ease. Or as much at ease as a man could be when he was staring down the barrel of a Colt Dragoon in the hands of someone who had just shown he knew how to use it.

Calhoun didn't believe him, but he nodded and uncocked the revolver. "Looks like your lucky day, Billy. Go on and follow the lady. Maybe if you catch her, you can get your share of her—and Quade's." He did not smile.

Billy nodded, more of his confidence returning. He was considerably relieved as he watched Calhoun holster the Dragoon. "Obliged, mister," he said. He turned and glided out of the door, shutting it behind him.

As soon as the door clicked into place, Calhoun moved. He turned the lamp low and slid out of the chair. In two steps, he was in the corner to the left of the chair.

Suddenly the door slammed open, cracking inward. Billy leaped inside after having kicked the door in. He crouched, Colt pistol extended. Both hands were wrapped around the revolver's handle. He fired four times with almost no pause between each shot.

Three of the pistol balls ripped into the chair, sending pieces of stuffing flying. The fourth crashed through the window.

"Goddamn fool," Calhoun said quietly as silence returned. He fired the Dragoon twice.

The last thing Billy remembered was the chill that ran up his spine when he heard the two simple words from the dark corner of the room. It was rather a shock as the two bullets ripped into his innards. He felt himself fall.

Calhoun quickly checked his work. As he had thought, both shots had been dead on. Calhoun leisurely wandered out of the room and closed the door behind him. As he passed the counter out front, he casually tossed the room key on it.

The sound awoke the old man briefly. He grumbled something and went back to sleep.

Calhoun walked outside into the snowy night.

CHAPTER

* 22 *

Wade Calhoun rode out of Cimarron shortly after dawn that day. The wind shrieked, whipping the light snowfall into a freezing, biting curtain.

Calhoun pulled his coat a little closer around him and scrunched his neck, trying to get as much of his head down into his coat as possible.

He had a bandanna tied around his face, from his nose downward, and his hat was pulled down to his eyebrows, but still the wind-whipped snow peppered him, stinging any bit of exposed flesh it could reach.

He had also tied a scarf around the top of his hat and under his chin. Not only did it keep his hat from blowing off in the gale, it kept his ears from freezing. With the thick leather gloves and his heavy flannel-lined canvas coat, he was as warm as he could be in a blizzard.

Amanda had been rather standoffish with him when he had returned to the rooming house after solving the problem of Rance Quade and Billy. She had stood by quietly and watched him begin packing his saddlebags.

"Where're you going?" Amanda had asked, interested despite herself.

"To get Nichols," Calhoun snapped.

"It's the middle of winter."

Calhoun said nothing.

"And a blizzard is blowing up."

"Don't matter." Calhoun gently moved Amanda out of his way as he pulled his only extra shirt out of the dresser drawer.

"It does to me." Amanda was shocked she had said that. But it was out now and there was no taking it back.

Calhoun stopped and looked at her in surprise. "I thought you didn't give a hoot about me one way or the other."

"I don't," Amanda said defensively. She was still in her nightshirt, though she had put furry slippers on her feet and wrapped a wool shawl around her shoulders.

"But I don't want to see you get killed out in a blizzard either," she added.

"These're the men who . . ."

"I know who they are," Amanda snapped. Tears and anger glistened in her eyes. "And, Lord knows I want them to pay for what they did. But you dyin' in a snowstorm ain't gonna bring them to justice."

Amanda began to sob now. All the trials and tribulations of the past several months were weighing on her, coming to a peak.

Calhoun stopped in front of her. He placed his big, hard hands on her shoulders and she looked up at him, tears staining her face. Her lower lip trembled. It hurt Calhoun to see her this way, and it brought back memories that were best forgotten.

"This is business that I should've taken care of a long time ago," Calhoun said slowly. He was not one for making speeches, but he felt a need to explain himself to Amanda at least a little.

"But I failed." The words were clipped with self-loathing. The thought of his still-recent wounds disgusted him. He had been an utter fool, and was lucky to be alive.

"You didn't . . ."

Calhoun placed a rough index finger across Amanda's soft lips, cutting off the flow of her words. "It's like a wound left untended too long," he said quietly. "If it ain't taken care of, it'll soon commence to festerin'. And once it's putrified, there ain't nothin' left to do but amputate."

He paused. He had already made a speech longer than he ever had, but he was not finished yet.

"I don't want this to get that far. I've got to take care of it now."

"It'll wait till spring," Amanda said reasonably. Her eyes searched his. She could see a deep, welling pain in those hard eyes. A pain from something that had happened. She knew she would never be able to plumb its depths or understand its meaning. She shuddered involuntarily.

Calhoun dropped his hands and turned away from her. "No, it won't," he said softly.

"Why?" Amanda asked, her voice pleading with him, seeking explanation.

Calhoun didn't want to explain. He had found that such things usually sounded lame under the best of circumstances. But he could see no way around it this time. He delayed long enough to roll a cigarette. He lighted it with the lantern.

Slowly, he turned to Amanda, thankful that she was a smart enough woman to have kept quiet while he thought of what to say. He sighed, blowing out a stream of smoke.

"Come spring, Garth Nichols is gonna ride back into Cimarron. And he ain't gonna be in a festive mood."

"How can you know that?" Amanda asked. Her eyes were imploring.

"I just know," Calhoun snapped. He wandered around the room, but there was little he could do. His few personal belongings were already in the saddlebags. All he needed were some foodstuffs and such. He could get those only at Blenheim's store. He would have to wait.

"So?" Amanda said, a challenge in her voice. "So what if Nichols comes back to town? You and Sheriff McCloskey can be ready for him then. You can set a trap." She paused, breathless with excitement as she thought of the possibilities.

"You said you killed four of them. There were only seven. You and some of the other men from town ought to be able to ambush the last three easy enough."

Damn, Calhoun thought. He wished others could see things as clearly as he could. Explaining was not his way. He faced her again. "Miss Amanda," he said slowly, revealing a little of his frustration, "Mister Becker is Nichols' half-brother. He told Nichols that I was after him. With four of his men dead, Nichols is gonna know I was the one who dusted 'em."

"So?" Amanda wondered what she was missing.

"Nichols ain't the kind of man to waste his time."

"But why . . .?"

"Because, dammit," Calhoun snarled, his exasperation getting the upper hand, "he'll be spendin' the winter recruitin' men to replace those he lost."

"How can you be sure of that?" Amanda asked. The thought was too frightening to contemplate.

"Because it's what I'd do was I in Nichols's shoes," Calhoun said firmly. He regained control of his emotions.

Amanda's horror grew. She began to imagine Garth Nichols returning to Cimarron with an army of slavering, well-armed desperadoes, all hell-bent on ruining the town and everyone in it. Especially Wade Calhoun. And herself.

"Oh, Lord," she groaned. Fear was gaining dominance over her other emotions.

Calhoun stepped up to her and enveloped her in his arms. He held her closely, stroking her long hair and her back. He knew she was scared stiff.

"Don't you fret now, Miss Amanda," he said softly after a little while. "It'll be taken care of."

Amanda sniffled against his chest.

"But that's why I've got to go out after him now," Calhoun added quietly. "Before he can hire new men."

Amanda sniffled a few more times. Then she turned her face upward. She looked at him with tear-gleaming eyes underscored by desire.

Calhoun bent his head and kissed her hard. She responded in kind, hungrily moving her lips. Calhoun managed to bend his knees and scoop her into his arms. She was as light as a feather. He turned toward the bed.

*   *   *

Amanda left the room only ten minutes before Sheriff McCloskey knocked on the door. Calhoun, who had dressed quickly, answered it cautiously, his pistol in hand.

McCloskey looked blandly at the Colt Dragoon that hovered inches from his belly. "Mind if I come in?" he asked sourly.

Calhoun uncocked the pistol, shoved it away and stepped back.

McCloskey entered the room slowly, leaving the door ajar. He made no comment, though Calhoun figured the lawman must suspect what had gone on in the room not so long ago. Calhoun rolled a cigarette, not saying anything.

"I've been busy," McCloskey said.

"Oh?" Calhoun's whole body radiated the indifference he felt.

"Yep. The gunplay here—and the body it left—started it all. I found Willy Becker beaten and then shot through the head, over in his billiards parlor. Found two more bodies shot dead over at the Cimarron Queen."

"So?" Calhoun still couldn't work up any enthusiasm. If McCloskey wanted to accuse him of something, he would deal with it. If not, then all he wanted to do was get rid of the lawman and get on with the job he faced.

"So, what do you know about all of it?"

"Nothin'."

"I'd hate to call a man like you a liar, Mister Calhoun," McCloskey said slowly. "But I find that a little hard to believe."

Calhoun shrugged. He didn't much care what the sheriff believed—or thought.

"Goin' somewhere?" McCloskey asked, pointing to the saddlebags on the chair.

"Maybe."

McCloskey paced the room a little, then stopped across the room from Calhoun and faced him.

"I ain't about to try tellin' you how to go about your business," he said tentatively. He knew he was treading on thin ice here, but he had to say what he had come to say.

He took off his hat and scratched his head. "And I don't reckon I could be of much help to you." He paused, twirling the hat he still held in hand. "But I'd be mighty obliged if you was to tell me what your plans were."

"Ain't your concern, Sheriff." There was no anger in Calhoun's voice, and no sympathy either.

"Maybe not," McCloskey admitted. "But . . . well, dammit, I know you had somethin' to do with all those killin's tonight." He held up his hand to forestall any possible protest, and to let Calhoun know he wasn't finished.

"It don't matter none either way. I doubt I could prove it. And even if I could, I expect nobody'd feel the worse for it. Except maybe Willy's wife." She was a timid mouse of a woman who would never cause any trouble.

"Still, I'll have to give some explanation for it all to the judge. I'd be more willin' to keep your name out of it if you was to let me know what you're plannin'."

Calhoun thought it over. He had no particular fond-

ness for John McCloskey, but the sheriff had helped
him in some small ways. Besides, the lawman was just
doing his job. Calhoun could see no reason not to tell
McCloskey of his plans unless McCloskey was somehow in cahoots with Nichols, which Calhoun figured
was highly unlikely.

Calhoun explained it in a few short sentences.
There was not much to tell anyway.

McCloskey looked relieved when Calhoun had finished. He saw the wisdom of the move. "I wish you
luck, then, Mister Calhoun," he said solemnly. He
meant it. If Calhoun were successful, Cimarron would
be rid of the Nichols problem. If not, the town could be
in serious trouble.

"Reckon I could use it," Calhoun allowed.

"You plannin' to come back to Cimarron?"

Calhoun caught a glimpse of Amanda watching
from just outside the door to the room. He shrugged.
"Ain't likely."

McCloskey nodded, accepting it. "Anything I can
do?" he asked.

"Nope."

McCloskey nodded again. He set his hat on and
marched out.

A few minutes later, Amanda Powell tapped on the
door and entered. "Did you mean it about not comin'
back?" she asked. Amanda looked composed. She had
dressed simply in a plain calico dress. Her hair was
done up.

"I reckon that'd be best, ma'am," Calhoun said
politely.

Amanda nodded. She had decided in the past half-hour that despite her deep feelings for Calhoun, she did not really love him. She also knew that life with him, while it might provide some hellaciously interesting times, would not be comfortable. There would always be the call of the trail; or the tug of his past. He would not be content to settle down and raise a family.

She would be better off without him, she knew. But she was glad she had met him. The past week had been quite out of the ordinary, and she would cherish it always.

Amanda had been almost relieved to hear him say he most likely would not be back in Cimarron again. It saved her from having to tell him she couldn't bear to see him again.

"Is there anything I can do for you before you leave?" she asked quietly.

A few lustful thoughts burst through Calhoun's head. He quelled them only with an effort. "You could roust old Blenheim and have him open his store. I'll be needin' some supplies."

"I expect it's the least I can do." She headed for the door. Halfway out, she stopped. She turned and strode boldly up to him. Resting her dainty hands on his hard arms, she stood on tiptoe and kissed him.

"Thank you," she breathed into his mouth. "For everything."

CHAPTER

* 23 *

Calhoun realized about halfway though Cimarron Canyon that he had been a goddamn fool for leaving on this quest in the teeth of a blizzard. But he would rather die out here amid the howling wind and screaming snow than turn tail and go back to Cimarron. Besides, he'd never make it back there anyway.

The only thing he would regret, though, about dying at the screeching hands of this monstrous storm would be not completing his job. He was sick at heart knowing that if he died, Garth Nichols and his band of cutthroats would descend upon Cimarron as soon as spring arrived. That would mean Amanda would suffer even rougher treatment than her mother had.

That thought kept him going as he pushed through the roaring gusts that smashed him off his horse more than once. Several times the mule had been battered down. Honking and braying, the beast always fought back to its feet. Calhoun began to believe the mule had as much gumption as he had himself. And as little brains, considering their situation.

Seeing in his mind's eye Amanda being ravaged by Nichols' men drove him cursing and stumbling and fighting through the storm. He lost track of time and distance. Only his obsession with finding and killing Garth Nichols, Harry Graham, and Conley Muir—and anyone else Nichols might have hired on—had any reality for him.

Visions swam before his eyes, dancing on the spinning, darting clouds of stinging snow. He saw a farm in Kansas Territory, with wheat and tall prairie grass bending under the gentle summer breeze. He saw a woman, tall, willowy, beautiful. And a little girl, a bundle of gurgles and toothless smiles. He saw painted savages on horseback and then blood, flames, and death. Always death.

"Shit!" Calhoun roared as a new burst of wind knocked his horse over on its side. The word was torn from his lips by the whirlwind and whisked away into the distance.

He managed to grab the horse's reins as the animal bucked and jerked upward. The bay tried to bolt, but Calhoun was able to pull himself into the saddle by sheer arm strength after he had been dragged several yards by the straining horse. The deep snow kept the steed from gaining too much speed, which made Calhoun's job a little easier.

"Goddamn stupid animal," he shouted, knowing the horse could not understand him, even if it could hear him with the wind roaring like it was. He yanked on the reins as hard as he could, jerking the beast's head around. "Hold up there, you stupid hoss!"

The horse pulled up, snorting and stomping. It champed at the bit.

"Just settle down, dammit," Calhoun mumbled. He patted the horse's neck where he could reach it. Calhoun was shaking a little, both from the cold and the exertion. Calhoun knew he was not up to full strength. That was bothersome. He also realized it was dangerous.

Calhoun looked around, trying to pick out a landmark, but he could see little in the swirling devilishness of the snowstorm. Vision was limited to less than ten yards.

He moved on, keeping the horse on a tight rein, angling a little to his left. He thought he had seen the dark fortress of trees that way. An hour later, he found the edge of the trees. He figured he had come a little more than a quarter of a mile.

He followed the ragged line of pines, searching for some kind of opening into the massed foliage. He finally found a small gap and edged the horse in.

It was not a path by any means, but the spacing of the trees was sufficient to let him pass. He wound deeper, enveloped in the eerie silence now that he was protected by the trees, which broke the sound of the wind for the most part.

Calhoun finally came upon a small, rough clearing amid the pine trunks. It was an oblong just about large enough to lay his bedroll. He stopped and looked up. The treetops bent close together forty feet above, blocking most of the snow. The trees and branches were so thick that they had kept the ground mostly dry here. A thick layer of pine needles covered the earth. Calhoun decided it was a good place to hole up and dismounted.

After tying the horse to a bough, he walked off between the trees. He found enough space between the trunks for the horse and mule to move about a little. Even a little brown grass was available. With the oats he had brought, he figured the two animals should be fed well enough. Unless he was here till spring, he thought wryly.

He was weakening rapidly, so Calhoun simply took what he needed off the mule. He quickly gathered a little firewood and built up a small blaze just to the edge of the "clearing." He put coffee on to boil and began frying up a passel of bacon.

He waited, trying to be patient. When the bacon was done, Calhoun ripped into it, bolting down chunks of the greasy meat. He knew the fat would help him stave off the cold and would build up his strength.

The coffee helped to warm him. By the time he had finished eating and polished off his fourth cup of sugary Arbuckle's, he was feeling a sight better. His arms and legs no longer trembled, and the sluggishness had sloughed off him.

He shoved himself up and went about his chores. There was not much to do, but what there was had to be done.

He unpacked the mule and curried the animal. Afterward he checked the mule over. Except for one rough spot on his back where the packs had rubbed too much, it appeared to be in good shape. Calhoun tied the mule to the tree with a good length of rope. He filled a feed bag with oats and hung it over the mule's muzzle.

Calhoun turned his attention to the horse. He unsaddled it, and rubbed that beast down, too. Calhoun had never taken to horses as almost pets like some men did. He simply saw whatever horse he had at the time as a tool. He could get along without one, if needed, though he hated being afoot. And he treated a horse as such, a tool to be cared for as well as possible, something not to be abused unless necessary to save his own neck.

This horse was a decent enough animal. It had shown some spirit during the ride through the storm and had not balked at anything he had asked of it. Because of that, it deserved good treatment. Nothing more.

After currying the horse, he checked it over. The shoe on the right foreleg appeared to be loosening some, which could become a problem. But Calhoun knew he didn't have far to go. If he ever got moving again.

He gave the horse a nose bag full of oats, and then went about gathering more firewood. The temperature was below zero already, and he figured it was going to get even colder. He wanted plenty of wood on hand.

Finally he sat on his spread-out blankets. He moved as close to the fire as he dared, though not right on top of it. Then he unloaded, cleaned, oiled and reloaded all his guns, one at a time.

When he was finished with that, he had a cup of coffee and a cigarette. He pulled the feed bags off the horse and mule and stowed them away. Turning in, he pulled the blankets close against the frigid night.

Calhoun began to think he would never be able to leave this place. The storm showed no signs of abating as the days passed. His food supplies began to dwindle, as did his close-by supply of firewood. He grew tired and lethargic, worn down by the cold and monotony.

He found the blotchy bay horse dead on the third morning, frozen to death.

"Shit," Calhoun mumbled, annoyance growing when he saw it. Not only was he irritated at the loss of the animal, he was angry at himself. He had never even heard the horse fall during the night. Such sluggishness could be fatal, he well knew.

He jumped up and down a few times, and paced his tiny campsite rapidly to get his blood moving. Once he had done that, he built up the fire and put on coffee and the last of his bacon. Then he checked the mule.

The beast looked to be in relatively good shape. It apparently had lost some weight since its food supply was not the best. But it seemed to be surviving. Calhoun took one of his blankets and tied it lightly around the mule. He didn't know if it would do any good, but he thought it couldn't hurt.

After eating his breakfast, Calhoun looked with distaste at the horse. He had no choice. All he had left was a half-pound of elk jerky and a small portion of smoked pork. He needed the meat.

Butchering the frozen horse carcass was not easy. The temperature never rose above ten degrees, so there was no chance for the meat to really thaw. Calhoun finally resorted to chopping out chunks with his hatchet. He wrapped the hunks in horsehide and hung the bundles by ropes as high up in trees as he could get them. He didn't need scavengers lurking about.

When he had gotten all the meat he thought he could use, Calhoun tied the remains of the horse to the mule. He walked away from the campsite, leading the mule. The animal calmly dragged the carcass along. It was tricky work, since the horse's legs—frozen by both the temperature and rigor mortis—kept catching in trunks and brush.

Calhoun left the bloody thing almost a mile from his camp, deep in the forest. He walked with the mule back to his camp. *What next?* he wondered as he poured himself another cup of coffee.

By that afternoon, he could hear a change in the wind that bent the tops of the pines. It slowed steadily, and by the next morning, the wind was a mere breeze. The snow had stopped.

Just to be on the safe side, Calhoun gave it one more day. Then he threw the saddle blanket and saddle on the mule and climbed aboard. The mule wasn't sure he liked this, but Calhoun growled at the animal and rode out.

Out in the open of Cimarron Canyon, the snow was piled belly deep to a horse in most parts. The screaming wind from the storm had swept other places almost bare of snow. The snow gleamed and glittered with crystalline brilliance in the weak sun. It hurt Calhoun's eyes. He cut slits in a bandanna and tied it around his face so he could see.

It was still colder than a banker's heart, but Calhoun had experienced such before.

Finding the road that ran east and west through the canyon was difficult, since virtually the entire canyon was deep in snow. But Calhoun decided he didn't really need a road. He just turned east at the first likely spot and rode on.

CHAPTER

✴ 24 ✴

Black Water was a dingy, grimy little town, like too many others Calhoun had seen in his short, violent life. It was a little bigger and better outfitted than Sierra, where Calhoun had gunned down Cridlow and the young man named Abe, but not much.

The brownish adobe and wood buildings huddled in impotent defiance of the elements. Snow was piled up—either by nature or by much shoveling—along the sides of many buildings. Icy ruts cluttered the street that meandered through the center of the town.

There was little activity in Black Water. Most of the people decided that staying inside was vastly preferable to walking the streets in the frigid afternoon air.

The four saloons Calhoun passed in the northern half of the town seemed to be doing a pretty good business. Noise and light erupted from all four, dispelling some of the gloom that had settled over Calhoun. He was sick of such bleak, backwater towns as this. He was tired of his mission, wanting it over and done with. He was tired of the bad luck and violence that dogged him, like homesick puppies.

Down a small, frozen side street, Calhoun spied a hotel sign. He shrugged and turned the mule in that direction. He stopped and dismounted in front of the place. The building looked forlorn. It was a place that had no better days to look back on.

The hotel sign hung by one hook, dangling, buffeted by every stray breeze that came along. As Calhoun moved toward the door—like the sign, painted red— he noticed that the adobe walls were cracked. A rat poked its head out of one larger hole in the wall, then ducked back inside.

Calhoun had to shove the door hard to open it. A small bell clanged when the door, swollen by the air's moisture, scraped open. The inside was as unprepossessing as the outside. A few ratty chairs were scattered about what was supposed to be a lobby. A rack with numerous slots for keys hung on the back wall. There was no counter, only a sagging desk in one corner.

A middle-aged man with a roll of fat around his midsection and a bulbous nose snored in a chair. His feet were on another chair.

With a look of disgust, Calhoun kicked the man's nearest foot. "Wake up, lard belly," he called.

The man jerked awake. Not looking at Calhoun, he rubbed both meaty hands over his flabby face. "What the hell do you want?" he asked, his tone surly.

"A room," Calhoun responded curtly.

"Is that any reason to go disturbin' a man's well-earned slumber?" the flabby man asked petulantly. He looked up for the first time, ready to berate whoever it was that had bothered him.

The fat man looked into Calhoun's cold, dark eyes and trembled. The flabby jowls quivered. He always had been a man to open his mouth before thinking of what he had to say. He had been lucky for forty-two years in that someone hadn't called him on it. Now, looking into those hard, glittering orbs, he thought the time had come.

"Sorry," he mumbled, worried. He made an attempt to hop out of his chair, to hastily do this stranger's bidding. He hoped that would keep him alive. But he couldn't make it, and settled for pushing himself ponderously up. He stood, wheezing from the effort.

Calhoun watched with disinterest, impatience mushrooming. He was tired, cold and hungry. He was frustrated in not having completed his task long ago. He was angry at the men who had sent him on this mission in the first place. And he was filled with self-disgust at having let himself be wounded before getting the job done.

All that left Calhoun in less than joyful spirits. This fat hotel keeper's plodding movements and humorless attitude did not offer any improvement in the way Calhoun felt, but he kept himself under control. He was virtually certain that he would find Garth Nichols and the others here in Black Water. If that were true, his mission would soon be over.

The hotel keeper waddled to the desk. Though the wind rattled in through the holes and cracks of the building, chilling the lobby, the man wiped sweat off the rolls of fat on his neck. He dipped a pen into an inkwell and held it out.

With a shrug, Calhoun took the pen. He indifferently scrawled his name in the book where indicated by the hotel keeper's blubbery finger. He dropped the pen on the book and fished a coin out of a trouser pocket and placed it next to the pen. "The key," he said flatly.

The portly hotelier grabbed a key and held it out. "Upstairs, out front."

Gunfire erupted outside, as it had two other times since Calhoun had ridden into Black Water. Calhoun shook his head. "Give me a room at the back," he ordered.

The hotel keeper's bulbous head bobbed in acknowledgement. He rummaged in the slots behind him and pulled another key. Calhoun nodded and took the key. "Livery?"

"Across the street. Couple doors down." The fat man did not know why he was so frightened, just that it was growing steadily worse. Calhoun had made no move against him, had made no threats. Still, the hotel keeper was petrified. So much that his voice squeaked as it struggled out past his fat throat.

"There a man named Garth Nichols in town?" Calhoun asked, eyes boring into the other man's.

The blubbery shoulders lifted and fell. The man's pasty face paled even more.

Calhoun had picked up a new set of wanted posters on Nichols, Conley Muir, and Harry Graham before he had left Cimarron. He hauled the weathered, crumpled pieces of paper out of his pocket. He culled out Nichols's and shoved it under the fat man's gaze. "You seen him around Black Water lately?"

"Yes," the hotel keeper said, relieved. He hoped he could send this mean-looking *hombre* on his way soon. "Can't say as I know him though."

"Know where he's stayin'?"

"Nope." The man looked apologetic, and still scared.

"Where he spends his time?"

"Nope." The hotel keeper began to worry again.

Calhoun nodded. He had hoped the man might point him in the right direction. Since he had not, Calhoun's job would be a little tougher. But not much. A man like Garth Nichols would be likely to spend a considerable amount of his time in saloons and brothels. Calhoun did not mind visiting those places in search of his quarry.

"You serve food?"

"Nope." The man pointed a shaky, fat finger. "Down the main street. There's a restaurant. And Madame Ilona's place serves food. In addition to . . ."

"Obliged," Calhoun allowed. He jammed the room key into his coat pocket and went outside. It was still bitter cold, but the weak afternoon sun gleamed unhampered by clouds. Calhoun pulled his saddle, saddlebags and bedroll off the mule and carted the items up to his room.

It was a typical room. A small bed with plenty of covers and a heavy quilt. A single, rickety chair stood alongside an equally frail-looking table. A lantern sat on the table. A small stand next to the bed had a porcelain basin and pitcher. A small, cast-iron stove glowed in a corner.

Calhoun dropped his gear on the floor out of the way and then went downstairs. He rode bareback over to the livery and left the mule. He walked up the side street, past the hotel, to the main street. He turned left and headed up the main street.

He stopped at a chophouse and looked inside. Then he glanced across the street at Madame Ilona's. He opted for the bawdyhouse. He strolled over and went inside.

Judging by what he had seen so far, he figured that Madame Ilona's was one of the better places in town. That still did not make it fancy. The interior was white-washed adobe. Furniture was sparse, mostly couches and some mirrors. A worn rug covered the floor, and two stoves burned in opposite corners, boosting the temperature inside to an almost tolerable level.

The few couches scattered about the greeting room were bedecked by goose-pimpled, miserable-looking women. Most of them were young and not at all attractive.

A plump, overdressed woman with too much make-up approached him. She smiled. At least Calhoun assumed it was a smile; he could not be sure.

"Welcome," she said huskily. "I am Madame Ilona."

It was a voice that grated on Calhoun's nerves rather than instilling a sense of desire. "Evenin', ma'am," he said politely.

"See anything you like?"

"Several things," he lied. "But I expect some food'd be the first thing I'd want."

The plump woman nodded. "Afterward?" she asked hopefully. She made her money on her girls and served food only as a sideline. It was an enticement for the men to linger longer and spend more money on the girls.

"Reckon I can find somethin' to my likin' here, ma'am," Calhoun said.

Madame Ilona nodded and led him to a room off the main one. Half a dozen tables were set up there.

Calhoun took his time over the pork chops, yams and peas, followed by coffee and a cigarette. He figured business was slow, since Madame Ilona hovered near him throughout the meal. Finally he finished, and let himself be coaxed into visiting the parlor.

He picked out a tall, stout, not unpleasing woman who said her name was Lily. Calhoun paid his money, and he and Lily retired up the stairs to a small, uncomfortable room.

When they were through, Calhoun began dressing. He pulled the papers out of his shirt and tossed them on the bed. Lily still lay there, covers pulled up to her chin, not because of any modesty but because of the chill in the room.

"You ever seen any of those boys?" he asked.

Lily sat up, letting the covers fall. She had always been proud of her body, and liked to show it off. She picked up the papers and scanned them, nodding. "Seen all three at times."

"They come in here often?"

"No. Of a time, though."

"You know where they usually go?"

"The St. Joe Saloon." When Calhoun looked at her blankly, she climbed out of the bed. She took his hand and led him to the window and pointed up the street.

In the last of the day's sunlight, Calhoun saw a rough, adobe tavern. A large painted sign pronounced it the St. Joseph Saloon.

"The owner come from St. Joe, Missouri," Lily said by way of explanation.

Calhoun nodded.

Lily shivered from both the cold and from desire.

She looked up at him. "There's time for . . ." she said hopefully and nodded her head toward the bed.

"I'm low on cash," Calhoun said truthfully.

Lily smiled ruefully. He had been fun to be with, and she would have enjoyed another round with him, but giving it away was not her style. "Another time, sugar," she said. There was only a little regret in her voice.

"I'll be certain to look you up," Calhoun said glibly. He had no intention of being in town long enough for another visit to Madame Ilona's. He tipped his hat at her and strolled out the door.

Outside the brothel, he stopped. Darkness was just falling. The air was bitterly cold, but the sky was clear. He stepped off the bottom stair onto the icy street and turned south. He marched toward the St. Joe Saloon.

CHAPTER

* 25 *

Calhoun spotted Nichols as soon as he walked into the saloon. The outlaw sat with Muir, Graham, and two other men at a table made from several slabs of pine.

The saloon was a foul, grimy place. A pall of smoke hung just below the low ceiling. It was close and hot in the small saloon. Odors assaulted Calhoun's nostrils—sweat, unwashed men, vomit, urine, old tobacco and stale whiskey.

A burly ape of a man wearing a once-white apron stood behind what passed for a bar. The saloon's owner had taken a wagon he had been bringing from St. Joe and buried the wheels in the dirt about halfway up to the hubs. He had knocked the sides off the wagon and used it as a bar.

Calhoun took a few moments to survey the room after he closed the plain, double doors behind him. The place was busy but not overly so. All ten small tables were occupied and several more men stood at the makeshift bar. Three painted women circulated through the room, trying halfheartedly to drum up business.

No one seemed especially interested in Calhoun, though everyone had glanced up at the opening of the door.

Calhoun pulled off his gloves and stuffed them into his coat pocket. He tugged off the canvas coat and hung it on a peg next to the door. He wanted to be unfettered when the action started.

He felt a rush of excitement. Things were coming to a head. His quarry was in front of him, and a resolution was at hand.

He gave no thought to the five-to-one odds. He was confident in himself. He also had a fatalistic attitude. He knew he could die here soon, but he also knew that he would take all or most of his prey with him when he went under. That was all he hoped for.

He sauntered toward the table and stopped in the gap where a sixth chair could have fit. Nichols, directly across the table from Calhoun, glanced up. When he saw it was no one he knew, he dismissed the newcomer.

The four other men did likewise.

Muir was the nearest to Calhoun, on his right; a man Calhoun did not know sat between Muir and Nichols. On the other side, Graham sat next to Nichols, and another man unknown to Calhoun was on Graham's right.

The five men continued to studiously ignore Calhoun. They talked and gulped their whiskey. Calhoun knew they were well aware of him, though.

Calhoun hawked up some phlegm in his throat and spit. The foul glob landed on Nichols's shirt.

Four of the five men quickly moved their hands toward their guns, though no weapons were pulled.

Nichols simply looked up at Calhoun in amazement. Or maybe bemusement. The surprise in his eyes quickly gave way to a burning anger. His voice was calm as he asked, "What in hell'd you do that for, mister?"

"Get your attention."

"You got it." His lips curled in an angry sneer.

The other men relaxed, and most put their hands back on the table. All of them watched Calhoun intently.

"Now speak your piece, mister," Nichols said acidly. "And I'd suggest you make it good, since it's the last thing you'll ever say to anyone."

Calhoun's hand was a blur as he whipped out one of the Colt Dragoons. It swung out of the holster and stopped with the end of the muzzle brushing Muir's temple. Calhoun did not look at the man; he continued watching Nichols.

"You pull that piece, son, and your brains'll be splattered all over the floor before you get it halfway out."

Suddenly sweating, Muir eased his hand away from his pistol butt and set it on the table.

Calhoun nodded. After several long moments of letting Muir worry, he uncocked his Dragoon and holstered it.

"I'm a friend of Mother Agatha Powell," Calhoun said tightly, looking at Nichols.

"Who?" Nichols asked in mock innocence.

"The kindly woman you defiled—and then killed—over in Cimarron."

"I don't recall ever doin' such a thing," Nichols commented. He wore a look of bland unconcern.

"Lyin' ain't gonna save your miserable ass, Nichols. Not this time."

Time seemed to stand still, hanging in the air in anticipation. Sounds stopped as saloon patrons seemed to sense that something was about to happen.

Then there came a flashing burst of activity.

Calhoun snatched out both Dragoons from the cross draw holsters in a well-oiled move. He fired the one in his right hand.

The blast caught the unknown man sitting between Muir and Nichols in the forehead. He was blown back out of the chair, a large chunk of his head gone.

At the same time, Calhoun lashed out with the Dragoon in his left hand. The barrel cracked across the other unknown man's nose, at the bridge. The young man groaned. His blue eyes rolled up into his head and he fell out of the chair.

The same pistol jerked some inches back toward the table, and Calhoun fired it.

Harry Graham had moved fast. The hawk-nosed thug slid out of his chair to the side. With one hand he pulled a Colt; with the other, he shoved up on the table.

At the same time, Nichols, who had been hindered by the table in getting his pistols out, shoved the table up. With Graham's assistance, the table lifted, teetered a moment, and then toppled onto its side.

Nichols and Graham ducked behind it. As they did, Calhoun emptied the Dragoon in his left hand. Two slugs tore chunks out of the round edge of the heavy pine table. The last two plowed into the timber.

"Damn," Calhoun swore silently. He swung to his right.

Muir had fallen out of his chair. He had hit harder

than he had expected. The blow on his elbow numbed his arm temporarily, and he had trouble getting his pistol out of the holster. Still lying down, he had finally managed, and gotten off a quick shot at Calhoun.

The saddle tramp felt the bullet tear through his shirt sleeve. As Calhoun dropped into a crouch and brought his pistol to bear on Muir, a bullet from behind the table sent his hat sailing across the room.

Calhoun fired twice at Muir, who was set for his second shot. One bullet cracked Muir's collarbone; the second drilled the outlaw in the top of the head, at the hairline.

Even as he was firing, Calhoun fell to his right and rolled several times. In the twirling chaos, he saw both Graham and Nichols pop up twice from behind the table and fire at him. Bullets kicked up clods of dirt floor where Calhoun had just been.

Calhoun heard a bottle break somewhere behind him. Then a man across the room yelped in pain. Calhoun figured the man back there had been shot.

Calhoun rolled to a stop and pushed up onto one knee. As Nichols stuck his head up again to fire, Calhoun let go his last two shots. Nichols ducked quickly.

Even as he jammed both empty pistols back into the holsters, Calhoun was shoving up. He ran crouched over, heading straight for the overturned table.

He had a momentary glance of Graham coming up over the table, pistol ready. Before the outlaw could fire, Calhoun slammed full force into the wide top of the table.

The blow shoved the heavy table back a few feet,

spilling Nichols and Graham on their backs. Calhoun jumped up and vaulted the table. His boots landed on Graham's right leg.

Graham howled with the pain of tearing ligaments. But he still managed to kick out with his left foot. The heel of his boot caught Calhoun behind the knee, and Calhoun fell.

As he fell, Calhoun spied Nichols scrambling around on the floor looking for his pistol. Calhoun could not worry about him now. He broke his fall with his arms, rolled once and came up.

Graham, who had beat Calhoun to his feet, tried to kick him in the face. The boot whistled within an inch of Calhoun's face. Calhoun made a futile attempt to grab the swinging leg. He missed, but Graham, standing on his damaged leg, was a little off-balance.

Calhoun leaped, slamming his shoulder into Graham. The two fell, hit hard and bounced apart. As they both struggled to their feet, Graham whipped his pistol out. The iron front sight nicked Calhoun's head and temple.

Calhoun was too full of adrenaline to feel the short, sharp pain of the glancing blow. Enraged, he tried to kick Graham in the crotch, but missed. His boot sloughed off Graham's left thigh. It didn't hurt Graham much, but it did throw his aim off as Graham fired his pistol.

The saddle tramp lunged at Graham again. The outlaw swung his empty pistol at Calhoun's head once more. Calhoun managed to get his left arm up and block the blow. Graham dropped the pistol in the collision of arms.

The two men grabbed each other and grappled. As Graham tried to butt Calhoun's face with his forehead, Calhoun jerked out of the way. Using his depleted, but still-considerable strength, he tugged Graham around. That left Graham's back to Nichols.

Calhoun had been somewhat worried that the outlaw leader would grab his pistol and cut loose. He just hoped that Nichols would not want to shoot Graham, whom Calhoun had heard was Nichols's lieutenant, in the back.

Calhoun could feel himself weakening. He was not worried about losing the fight, or even dying so much. What bothered him was the possibility of having come so far and not being able to complete the task he had set for himself.

The possibility of failure gave him a boost of energy. He flung Graham loose. Graham stumbled to the side a few steps. His damaged knee gave out and he began to fall. Calhoun helped him out by kicking him in the face.

Graham moaned as his jaw shattered, and he slumped.

Calhoun pulled his bowie from the shoulder rig. He figured to leap on Graham and finish him off in a hurry.

Then he heard someone roar, "You son of a bitch!"

Calhoun turned to see Nichols, kneeling, with his pistol cocked. Calhoun figured he was done for, but he was not going to give up easily. He spun on his heel and dived, hoping to make the cover of the heavy table a few feet away.

Nichols pulled the trigger. Nothing happened.

Calhoun landed hard on his stomach. He grunted

but did not wait. He crawled forward, heading for the table, not realizing that no bullets were hitting around him.

Nichols pulled the trigger again and again. Still nothing happened.

Calhoun had found haven behind the table. He wondered why he heard no gunshots. Then he heard a thunk on the table. He cautiously poked his head over the rim.

Looking stricken, Nichols had thrown his empty pistol at Calhoun. It hit the table as he jumped up and ran.

Calhoun saw Nichols fleeing. His first thought was to chase him, but then he realized that the outlaw could not get too far. Calhoun turned and looked at Graham.

The desperado had stood, standing gingerly on his hurt leg. His jaw was cocked all out of shape, and pain was in his eyes. He was not going to quit yet either. He pulled his own blade, a wicked-looking Arkansas Toothpick.

Graham tried to issue a verbal challenge, but his mangled jaw wouldn't allow it. He settled for a strangled moan and waving his hand in invitation.

Calhoun nodded, accepting. A red film of rage seemed to have settled over his eyesight. He could see no honor or bravery in the outlaw's challenge to him. And he could expect no honorable behavior in this fight to the death and he would not give any either. He wanted this over as quickly as possible.

Calhoun stalked forward slowly, knife weaving a pattern in front of him. Graham waited, crouched.

As Calhoun neared Graham, he suddenly spit in Graham's face. The outlaw flinched instinctively.

Calhoun used the opportunity to attack. He jumped to the side, then lashed out with a foot. His boot heel slammed against Graham's damaged knee.

Graham swore through his wrecked jaw and collapsed. He hit on his side but rolled over onto his stomach. As he pushed up with his arms, Calhoun suddenly straddled Graham's back.

Calhoun grabbed a handful of Graham's greasy hair and pulled back. The outlaw's head came back, exposing the throat. Calhoun's blade made a fast, short arc.

Blood spurted from Graham's severed carotids like water from a broken fire hose. Graham made a few odd, gurgling noises and then went silent.

Calhoun let Graham's limp head fall. He wiped his blade carelessly across the back of Graham's shirt several times, then put the clean knife back into his dangling sheath.

Calhoun stood. He surveyed the room with a quick sweep of his eyes. The patrons looked on in varying degrees of fear or disinterest. He saw no hate for him there. No love, either. But he figured that no one would make a play against him.

He walked to the one man of the four outlaws still in the room and living, the young man he had buffaloed with his pistol. The youth was coming to. He lay on the floor, blood trickling down from the bridge of his nose. His eyes were glazed.

"You fell in with the wrong boys this time," Calhoun said coldly. He pulled his bowie and plunged it into the man's heart.

Calhoun had no qualms about what he had just done. The young man had nothing to do with Mother Powell's rape and murder. But given half a chance, he would have. And would do so in the future, considering the men he had fallen in with. Calhoun had seen plenty of men like this before. He could see no good reason for the young man to go on living.

Once more Calhoun cleaned his blade on a victim's shirt and slid it safely away. He took one more glance around the room to make sure no one would object to what he had just done.

Then he spun and ran for the door. Hatless and coatless, he burst outside.

CHAPTER

* 26 *

Calhoun heard a commotion up the street and swung his head that way. About fifty yards away, Nichols had a hold of a horse's reins. A man on the horse was yelling as Nichols tried to work around to the side of the horse to pull the man down.

Calhoun began running toward them, his boots slipping on the slick city street.

The horse reared up, knocking Nichols to the side. Nichols swung his head around as he fell. Even at forty yards away, in the dark, Calhoun could see the panicked look on the outlaw's face.

Scrabbling for a purchase on the slick frozen ground, Nichols tried to roll and crawl out of the way as the horse slammed iron-shod hooves down on the ground. Little sprays of ice chips flew in all directions.

The horse's rider tried frantically to control the rampaging steed. He was having little success as the palomino gelding bucked and jumped. Plumes of vapor rolled out in frosty clouds from the animal's flared nostrils.

Nichols managed to roll out of the way, and suddenly the horse bolted. It raced up the street, mane flying. Its rider still tried desperately to both hold on and bring the charging animal under some kind of control.

The horse flew by Calhoun, almost knocking him down. Calhoun slipped on a slick spot, but it slowed him only a little. He kept running toward Nichols.

The outlaw made it to his feet. He spun as if to run, but then he stopped. He slowly turned to face the rushing Calhoun. He wiped ice and dirty snow off his clothes. His breath puffed out visibly in quick little clouds.

As Calhoun roared to within ten feet, Nichols suddenly bent and whipped a knife out of his boot. The foot-long dagger glittered evilly in the brittle silver moonlight.

"Shit," Calhoun mumbled. He tried to halt his headlong rush, but the frozen, ice-coated ground betrayed him. His boots slipped and skittered, and his arms flapped as he tried to keep his balance.

At the last minute, he let himself go down. He hit hard and his momentum slid him across the icy ground. His boots slammed into Nichols's ankles.

Nichols's feet went out from under him, catching him by surprise. He had no chance to stop himself. He fell atop the slowing, but still sliding Calhoun. As Nichols landed, Calhoun smashed an elbow into his face.

Nichols grunted as his nose bent and almost cracked. He fell to the side. Both men rolled to a halt, a few feet from each other. They hurriedly scrambled up.

They stood, breathing hard. Too much had happened to both in too short a time. It was barely three minutes since Calhoun had walked up to Nichols's table in the St. Joe Saloon.

"What's this old lady to you, anyway, mister?" Nichols asked, voice popping out in bursts.

"Just a friend." The fight had served to remove the rage from Calhoun—at least temporarily. He had been too distracted by the action to give anger much thought. But now the mere mention of Mother Powell by this vile, sadistic outlaw was enough to redraw the curtain of fury across his eyes.

"Friend," Nichols snorted in derision. He simply could not understand such things. To him, a woman was there for one reason. It made no difference that she might be old enough to be his mother. She had been reasonably attractive and available, even if she was taken by brute force. It was the only way he knew.

"Yep." Calhoun was keeping himself on a tight rein. His rage was close to erupting. He did not want that. He wanted to savor this man's death. He slid the big bowie out.

"Time for your comeuppance, boy," Calhoun snarled.

"Hell, I'm all a tremble." Nichols' voice was drenched with the scorn he felt for Calhoun.

The saddle tramp sprang. His big blade made short, wicked arcs as Calhoun slashed viciously at his opponent.

Nichols gave way slowly, then more rapidly, under the ferocious onslaught. Suddenly, he found himself with his back against the rough adobe wall of the hardware store. He braced for the final defense, certain he would be dead within moments.

Then Calhoun hit a large, solid patch of ice. His feet went out from under him, and he fell, cursing. He threw out his hands to catch himself. He hit hard, and the knife skittered free. He landed on his hands and knees.

Nichols wasted no time. He took one step forward and launched a boot at Calhoun's face.

Calhoun jerked his head to the side, and the kick caught him only a glancing blow.

Nichols stumbled a little after his foot came down, and he twirled. He made the move rather slowly, wanting to make sure he kept his footing. He came around, on Calhoun's left side just behind his shoulders. He raised the dagger and plunged it toward Calhoun's back.

Calhoun flopped flat onto his belly. Nichols's dagger nicked his back high up on the shoulder and slid downward, leaving a small, bloody trail. Calhoun rolled over onto his back, whipping out his legs at the same time. His boots knocked Nichols's feet out from under him.

Nichols fell on his buttocks, wincing at the sharp pain. He dropped the dagger.

Still lying on the frigid ground, his back rapidly getting chilled through the knife slit, Calhoun kicked at Nichols's head. He hit only the shoulder, but it tumbled Nichols over on his back.

Calhoun sprang up. As Nichols tried to rise, Calhoun slammed a hard fist into the side of the outlaw's face, knocking him over again. Then Calhoun slipped once more and went down himself again.

Calhoun knew he was running out of steam as he scrambled up. But he noted that Nichols was not moving as spryly as he once had either. Despite the bitterly cold temperatures, both men were sweating. They stood a moment, eyeing each other, trying to find a reservoir of strength. There was no sympathy in the eyes of either man, or respect. Only hate and revulsion.

Just the sight of the outlaw, and knowing what he had done to Mother Powell, built up the rage inside Calhoun again. He roared and charged. He crashed into Nichols, almost knocking him down then slammed a forearm into the outlaw's face, breaking his nose.

As Nichols staggered backward, Calhoun grabbed his shoulders and flung him.

Nichols was sent twirling, unable to gain his balance. Calhoun lunged at him again, smashing another forearm to the side of Nichols's head. Nichols fell back, limbs flailing helplessly. He crashed into the window of Heinz's Hardware store, sending shards of glass spraying over the street and the inside of the store.

Calhoun reached inside and grabbed Nichols by the shirt. He yanked him up. The outlaw came forward, seemingly limp. But as his feet landed flat on the ground, Nichols lunged. His forehead smashed into Calhoun's jaw.

"Dammit!" Calhoun burst out, startled. He lurched backward. His momentum was increased when Nichols punched him twice on the side of the face.

Calhoun's feet slipped and he fell, cracking his head on an ice puddle. It left him dazed.

"Son of a bitch," Nichols snarled. He grabbed Calhoun's shirt, and pulled him up. Holding him by a hank of shirt in his left fist, Nichols pummeled Calhoun.

The saddle tramp dodged his head, managing to avoid the worst of the punches. Regaining his senses a little, he managed to cover up and then land a few shots of his own.

"Bastard," Nichols growled. He hit Calhoun as hard as he could, letting go of the saddle tramp's shirt at the same time.

As Calhoun fell back, Nichols rammed his shoulder into Calhoun's midsection, knocking him backward with accelerated speed. Calhoun's back slammed against the hard adobe wall of the hardware store. It knocked the breath out of him.

Nichols smashed punches on Calhoun. The outlaw smelled victory—and another man's death. It gave him an impetus, a renewed viciousness.

Calhoun tried to cover up as best he could. His strength was sapped by the wounds he had suffered only two months ago, the storm, and this night's battle. He could feel himself fading out.

Suddenly, a vision appeared. The sight of kindly Mother Powell being ravaged by this slavering miscreant and his pack of jackals sent a surge of renewed power through Calhoun.

As he used his left arm to try fending off Nichols's driving blows, Calhoun's right hand was frantically scrabbling behind him. In the small space he managed to create between his back and the store's wall, he shoved his hand inside the slit shirt. He tore downward, fingers reaching desperately for his ace in the hole.

Finally he grabbed the butt of the spare pistol he always kept secreted. He snatched it out and jammed the two-inch barrel of the sawed-off Walker against Nichols's stomach.

Feeling himself fading in strength and consciousness, Calhoun pulled the trigger.

The blast of the short, blunt weapon was enormous. Calhoun had expected a big blast, but the rare chain fire of all five loaded chambers at once was astounding even to him.

The power of the explosion slammed Nichols backward several feet. His eyes registered shock for a moment. Then he fell. Most of his stomach, back and spine were gone. He landed in a collapsed heap, like a just-emptied bladder.

Calhoun leaned back against the wall. His chest heaved, and his breathing was hard through his damaged nose. He ached all over, and he was afraid to look at his torso, thinking he might have opened up his old wounds.

Black Water was silent, except for the rushing of the wind and the banging of a shutter somewhere. Even the dogs found it too cold to howl and bark and raise Cain.

A few men came out of the St. Joe Saloon and some other nearby places. They stood, gawking at the thin, powerful man leaning against the wall. They stared with repulsed awe at the mangled hunk of flesh that had moments ago been a hardcase named Garth Nichols.

The cold seeped into Calhoun's bones. He did not want to move and wasn't sure he could anyway. But he knew he had to—and soon—or he would die here against this wall. Besides, he would not give up in front of this rabble.

He shoved forward, surprising himself that he could stand straight. He shuffled a few steps, knelt cautiously and retrieved his bowie knife. He stood again and walked off.

Men parted and let him pass in silence.

Calhoun kept his head high as he walked back to the St. Joe. He would not let these townsmen see the pain he was experiencing.

He retrieved his coat and slowly began walking back toward his hotel. As he passed Madame Ilona's, Lily stepped out from the doorway. "Want company?" she asked.

"Another time, Lily."

Calhoun stopped the mule at the crossroads. A week had passed since his encounter with Nichols and the others. He had recovered considerably in that time. He had eaten well and spent two nights with Lily. That had cost him a pretty penny, but he figured it was worth it.

He had ridden out of Black Water that morning, several hours ago. The sky was dark with clouds, and the wind blew in gentle puffs of frigidness. He had no idea of where he was heading, only that he wanted to be away from Black Water.

As he stopped at the crossroads, snowflakes began to fall. He wondered for a moment which way to go. Black Water was fifteen or so miles behind him. Taos was twenty miles west; Cimarron about the same east.

He looked east, thinking of Amanda Powell. She had not indicated that she would welcome him back. But it would be tempting to see her again, he thought.

Then he sighed. He tugged on the mule's reins, and hit the road. He figured he would be in Taos well before dark.

CLINT HAWKINS is the pseudonym of a newspaper editor and writer who lives in Phoenix, Arizona.

Saddle-up to these

THE REGULATOR *by Dale Colter*
Sam Slater, blood brother of the Apache and a cunning bounty-hunter, is out to collect the big price on the heads of the murderous Pauley gang. He'll give them a single choice: surrender and live, or go for your sixgun.

THE REGULATOR—Diablo At Daybreak
by Dale Colter
The Governor wants the blood of the Apache murderers who ravaged his daughter. He gives Sam Slater a choice: work for him, or face a noose. Now Slater must hunt down the deadly renegade Chacon…Slater's Apache brother.

THE JUDGE *by Hank Edwards*
Federal Judge Clay Torn is more than a judge—sometimes he has to be the jury *and* the executioner. Torn pits himself against the most violent and ruthless man in Kansas, a battle whose final verdict will judge one man right…and one man dead.

THE JUDGE—War Clouds
by Hank Edwards
Judge Clay Torn rides into Dakota where the Cheyenne are painting for war and the army is shining steel and loading lead. If war breaks out, someone is going to make a pile of money on a river of blood.